Books by Michael Lister

(John Jordan Novels)
Power in the Blood
Blood of the Lamb
Flesh and Blood
The Body and the Blood
Blood Sacrifice
Rivers to Blood
Innocent Blood
Blood Money
Blood Moon
Blood Cries
Blood Oath

(Cataclysmos)
Cataclysmos Book 1
Cataclysmos Book 2

(Remington James Novels)
Double Exposure
Separation Anxiety

(Merrick McKnight Novels)
Thunder Beach
A Certain Retribution

(Jimmy "Soldier" Riley Novels)
The Big Goodbye
The Big Beyond
The Big Hello
The Big Bout
The Big Blast

(Sam Michaels and Daniel Davis Series)
Burnt Offerings
Separation Anxiety
Blood Oath

BLOOD Oath

a John Jordan Mystery

Book 11

by Michael Lister

Pulpwood Press
Panama City, FL

Inquiries should be addressed to:
Pulpwood Press
P.O. Box 35038
Panama City, FL 32412

Lister, Michael.
Blood Oath / Michael
Lister.
-----1st ed.
p. cm.

ISBN: 978-1-888146-67-7 Hardcover
ISBN: 978-1-888146-68-4 Paperback

Book Design by Adam Ake

Printed in the United States

1 3 5 7 9 10 8 6 4 2

First Edition

For
Betty Holloway
and
Veronica Carter

As I bring this series to my home town of Wewahitchka,
I can think of no better examples of the best of
Wewahitchka than these two amazing ladies.

Thank You

Dawn Lister, Jill Mueller, Mike Harrison, Don Minchew, Les Greenwood, Terry Lewis, and Aaron Bearden.

Author's Note

The John Jordan series is just that—a series. And should be read as such. I write each book in such a way as to avoid spoilers of previous entries and to prevent faithful readers from being subjected to endless recaps. Because of this approach, the series can be read out of order—but it also means that questions raised in this book will be answered in the books that came before it.

Blood Oath is the first John Jordan novel to feature characters from my other series.

If you haven't already, I recommend that you read *Burnt Offerings* and *A Certain Retribution* before reading *Blood Oath*.

There are other Merrick McKnight/Reggie Summers and Samantha Michaels/Daniel Davis novels, of course, but they aren't as pertinent to *Blood Oath*.

In the same way that reading the first ten John Jordan books before reading this latest one will greatly enhance your experience with and enjoyment of it, reading *Burnt Offerings* and *A Certain Retribution* first will be similarly beneficial.

But it's just a gentle suggestion. Nothing more. It's certainly not necessary. It will just answer questions raised in this book and reveal far more about these characters and their relationships and experiences. You could always read the others after reading *Blood Oath*. Or not at all—though I hope you won't choose this last option.

Regardless, I truly hope you enjoy John's latest adventure and the new direction his life is taking him. I certainly am.

Thank you very much for reading and for continuing to take this journey with me and John.

Blood Oath

Chapter One

Shane McMillan goes missing on the sweetest day of the year—the third Saturday in May, the day dedicated to celebrating the year's honey harvest at the annual Tupelo Festival in Wewahitchka—the tiny town that is the tupelo capital of the world.

The morning is bright, cool, and clear.

A beautiful day. The kind when nothing bad should be able to happen.

Beneath the enormous canopy of ancient live oak trees, the breeze blowing off Lake Alice waves the Spanish moss about and wafts around the savory smells of stir fry, barbecue, chargrilled chicken, sausage, burgers, and hotdogs, fresh fried catfish and grouper, and funnel cake.

Thousands of people fill the little lakeside park. Some winding their way around the cement walking track, slowly moving from vendor to vendor, lifting and examining and talking about the bottles of honey, homemade candles, kids clothes, wooden toys, wind chimes, hand-painted signs, scarves, and glass jars of special spices and sauces. Others sitting beneath the green tin roof of the pavilion listening to live music. Still others standing in line for food or sitting beneath the shade of a pole barn at picnic tables eating it. Some parents watch their kids play games, ride ponies, and jump in the bouncy castle in the middle of it all, while others look on as their kids swing and slide and climb on the permanent playground equipment at the far end. Politicians pass out campaign cards, brochures, T-shirts, and buttons. And, of course, competing commercial tupelo producers hawk honey like the golden nectar of the gods it is.

Anna and I and our two girls are right here mixed up in the middle of it all, soaking in the sights and sounds and smells, seeing people we haven't seen in years, meeting our new neighbors and citizens.

This is our home now.

Everything has changed.

Everything.

Well, everything but the most important things. Anna and I are together. Our daughters are healthy and well.

But everything else has changed.

We have moved, taken new jobs, are now a family of four.

We now live in Wewa. Anna now has a legal practice. I am now a chaplain at Gulf Correctional Institution and an investigator with the Gulf County Sheriff's Department. We now have two young girls—Anna's seven-month-old daughter, Taylor Elizabeth Taunton, and my four-year-old daughter, Sarah Johanna Jordan. Of course, they are only mine and hers by blood and birth. By every other measure, in every way that truly matters, they are both *ours*.

We are Wewahitchkaians.

Less than half an hour from Pottersville, Wewa is an awful lot like it—as are all the small towns and rural routes

14

in this part of North Florida.

Growing up, Anna and I both spent a good deal of time here. We both had family here. We both dated people from here back in high school. And we both always had a fondness for this place where so many of our friends live.

As we walk around the festival, each of us holding our daughter on our hip, we receive many warm congratulations for the wisdom we have displayed in moving to this great place.

They told us the same thing at the carnival in the old school yard last weekend and at our brief appearance at the softball tournament at TL James Park the weekend before.

"I like it here," Anna says to me. "A lot."

"Me too."

Tall and athletic with longish brown hair and big brown eyes, Anna still projects strength and beauty, but she's a bit more vulnerable than she's ever been before—because of both the brutal assault she had been subjected to and the distress she had suffered giving birth to Taylor.

"It really does feel like a new life."

"It is," I say.

After what we had been through—particularly her—we needed a new beginning. The physical trauma she had suffered alone was enough to warrant it, but she had been through enormous emotional turmoil as well.

"I just feel so damn hopeful and happy," she says.

"Me too," I say, reaching over and touching her face tenderly.

Across the way, through the throng, I can see Reggie Summers and Merrick McKnight.

They are heading this way and we walk toward them. Reggie Summers is Gulf County's first female sheriff and my boss. Merrick McKnight owns and operates the local paper, the *Gulf County Breeze*, and his family's beekeeping business, McKnight Apiaries, since his dad passed away at the end of last year.

"Sheriff," I say to Reggie.

She smiles. "Still haven't gotten used to that."

Reggie is an early forties country girl with a powerful five-nine frame, striking blue-green-gray eyes, straight saddle-brown hair perpetually in a ponytail, and olive skin. As if a uniform, I've never seen her in anything but blue jeans, boots, and a button-down.

If Anna has the build of a volleyball player, Reggie has the body of a softball player—the respective sports each woman excelled at in high school.

"Better hurry up," Merrick says with a rueful smile.

He's a little taller than Reggie, with intense eyes and a gentleness about him.

"That's true," she says. "Won't have it long. If I don't embrace it now I'll never get to."

Reggie has been appointed to her position by the governor and is under no illusion that she could actually win the seat in an election.

Both Anna and I are about to say something about her chances and our support, but she quickly moves off the subject.

"My, what beautiful girls," Reggie says. "If they still had the Tupelo Queen competition, you two would have to share it. With your mom."

She's right. They are truly lovely. Simple, unadorned beauty.

"Whatta you say, Johanna?" I ask.

"Thank you," she says, her small voice soft and airy.

She probably has no idea what Reggie has actually said, but she knows the right response to my question.

She looks up at me with her enormously big brown eyes and smiles.

I smile back and feel as I always feel when I look into her precious little face—a complex mixture of pure love, undiluted joy, and a fierce desire to keep her safe and happy. Looking at her also always reminds me that she looks as though she could be my and Anna's daughter instead of my and Susan's.

"Such good manners, sweet girl," I say. "I love you."

"I love you, Daddy."

"Thank you," Anna says to Reggie. "That's so . . . You're very kind."

"This your first Tupelo Festival?" Merrick asks.

We both shake our heads.

"First as Wewahitchkaians," I say.

"Makes a difference," he says. "How's the house working out for you?"

We had bought and are living in and fixing up his dad's old house, a red-brick ranch-style house built in the late sixties located on the other lake in town, Julia—the sister to Alice—just across Highway 22, less than a football field away.

Wewahitchka—Wewa to everyone who lives here—is a Native American term that means water eyes, named for the two lakes in the center of town, Alice and Julia.

"Perfectly," Anna says. "We love it."

"Sorry again about your dad," I say.

"Thank you," Merrick says, averting his gaze momentarily, blinking, clearing his throat. "It's amazing how many times a day I pick up my phone to call him or start to drop by and check on him. Don't be surprised if you open your door and I'm standing there sometime."

"You'd be welcome anytime," Anna says.

"Speaking of dads," Reggie says, "I had a thought about yours, John."

"Oh yeah?"

This past November, my dad lost his bid for re-election as sheriff of Potter County—the first time in decades—and has been adrift ever since, stuck in a sort of self-imposed purgatory.

"How do you think he'd feel about being a mentor and consultant for our department?" she says.

"Really?"

"I couldn't pay him much, but—"

It's the badness and brutality that gets the coverage and attention, but there is goodness all around us all the time.

"That's so extremely thoughtful of you," I say. "I'm sure he'd love to do it. And it'd be so good for him."

"He'd be a real asset for us, for me," she says. "I could really use a mentor."

"See?" Anna says. "That's why we need more women in office. No macho, ego, id bullshit to keep them from asking for help."

I nod. "Exactly."

Merrick nods his agreement.

"I'll talk to him about it," I say. "Thank you again. I know just being asked will do a lot for him."

"Well, we better check on our booth," Merrick says.

He has a booth set up to sell tupelo honey and *Gulf County Breeze* subscriptions.

"How was the flow this year?" I ask.

18

The tupelo flow—the narrow window when the tupelo trees bloom each year, usually less than two weeks—is a very delicate, fragile, and vulnerable event. Too much rain, too little, temperature changes, all affecting how much pure tupelo the bees can produce.

"Not as good as we had hoped," he says, frowning and shaking his head.

"Really?" Anna asks. "Thought the weather was perfect this year."

"Seemed like it, which is why we were so hopeful, but it got pretty cool a couple of nights. Think maybe that had something to do with it. Or I could've done something wrong. This is my first year doing it by myself. Still, we did okay. Stop by and get a jar before you leave."

We say we will and part ways with them.

"It's time to get your girls some vendor food," Anna says, flashing me a sweet smile beneath wide eyes.

"What would you like?"

"Some of all of it," she says. "It all looks and smells so good."

"What would you like to start with?"

"Surprise me."

While she takes both girls to find us a spot at a shaded picnic table, I go in search of food.

Food trucks and trailers are side by side with E-Z Up canopy tents—the latter used by local churches and school groups, such as Project Graduation. Behind them all, smoke from open-flame grills wafts up to hang in the tree branches above us.

I decide on fried fish dinners for us and chicken nuggets for Johanna.

Shane McMillan is in line when I walk up. He turns

toward me as I approach.

His hair is closely cropped in a military-style buzz cut, his nineteen-year-old body lean and muscular, his blue eyes bright and clear and penetrating.

"Hey," he says. "Do I call you Chaplain or Detective?"

"John," I say.

He smiles a big, warm, toothy smile and extends his hand. His handshake is what you'd expect from a young man in Ranger training at Fort Benning.

"No, sir. My mama would've never gone for that," he says. "How about Mr. Jordan?"

As a young teen, he had lost both his parents to different but equally lengthy and brutal illnesses.

"How's your training going?" I ask. "I'm surprised you got a weekend off."

"Don't get many, that's for sure. It's going good. I like it a lot. Plan to make a career out of it."

"That's great. What's Megan think about that?"

Megan Stripling is his girlfriend of several years. One year younger than him, she'll be a senior at Wewa High this year.

"She's not happy about it—or any of it, really, but we broke up," he says. "Or we're about to. That's the real reason I came home this weekend."

I nod. "Sorry," I say.

His bright blue eyes glisten a little and he blinks several times. "Thank you, sir. It'll be okay. It's for the best."

"I know you have Tommy, but let me know if you need to talk or—"

"I will, but I'm okay. Really. Thank you."

"How *is* Tommy?" I say, just to be saying something.

20

Tommy McMillan, Shane's older brother, is one of Anna's favorite cousins, a youth minister here in town, and the one who raised Shane after their parents passed away.

"He's good. He and Michelle are around here somewhere."

"I'll look for them," I say.

But I don't have to. They are sitting at the same table as Anna and the girls when I walk up with the food.

"Look who I found," Anna says.

"Hey John," Tommy says.

"Hey man. How's it going? I just saw Shane."

"He's supposed to be grabbing us some food," Michelle says.

Tommy and Michelle McMillan are in their midthirties but look younger. His hair is stylishly long, hers stylishly short. They're dressed more like teens than thirtysomethings. He's ruggedly hip with beard stubble and bright blue eyes. She's striking with a sharply angular face and eyes so dark they appear to be pupilless pools of blackness. They're youth ministers, but he looks like a musician, she like a primetime news anchor.

I place the chicken nuggets down in front of Johanna and begin pulling them apart to let them cool.

Anna opens the food container with one hand while giving Taylor small spoonfuls of pureed carrots with the other.

The open container reveals fried catfish filets, hush puppies, coleslaw, and baked beans.

Anna enthusiastically nods her approval. "Excellent choice. Good job there, Mr. Jordan."

"Will she let me feed her while y'all eat?" Michelle asks.

"Are you sure?" Anna says.

"Are you kidding?" Michelle says.

She and Tommy have been unable to have children, and though half the town's teens have adopted them, there is an essential if subtle sadness about them. Anna and I have always believed it's why Tommy remains a youth minister after all these years.

I stand and lift Taylor from Anna's lap to hand her to Michelle, but Tommy intercepts her on the way.

"Me first," he says, kissing her forehead. "Just for a minute. Do you mind?"

"Yes, I mind," Michelle says with a smile.

"You can feed me," Johanna says.

"I'd love to feed you," Michelle says.

"Me first," Tommy says.

Johanna beams.

While they fuss over and love on our girls, Anna and I eat together without having to do anything else—a true rarity these days.

"God, I love it here," she says.

"Me too."

"You know what we should do," Michelle says. "We should keep these angels one night each week for you two to have a date night."

"I'm only here on the weekends," Johanna says in her soft, sweet voice.

"Then we'll have to do it then," Michelle says. "Deal?"

"Deal."

Shane walks up with containers of food and sets

them on the table near Tommy and Michelle.

"Mission accomplished," he says.

"Thank you, Private," Tommy says.

"Aren't they just the cutest dorks you've ever seen?" Michelle says.

It is then I realize that in many ways Shane is more like a child than a brother to them.

"Permission to be dismissed, sir," Shane says.

"Where're you wanting to be dismissed to?"

"The river, sir." All roads lead to the river and one dead ends into it. "Me and Cody and Matt are gonna go to the end of the road and swim and hang out a while. We'll be back up here later this afternoon before everything's over."

The end of the road is what everyone around here calls Gaskin Park, the place where Lake Grove Road ends at the Apalachicola River.

"Good, 'cause here's where we're having dinner tonight," Michelle says. "So don't miss it."

"I won't."

"Have you talked to Megan, yet?" Tommy asks.

"Not yet, but—"

"Shane, you need to quit putting it off," he says. "You're not doing her right. Word's gonna get back to her and you're going to wind up hurting her, and I know you don't want that."

"Yes, sir. No, I don't. I'll do it as soon as we get back. Promise."

Cody and Matt meander up, the distinct hint of pot coming with them.

"See y'all later," Shane says.

"Shane," Tommy says. "Be careful. Respect the river.

Respect your future."

"He's an Army Ranger," Cody says. "Can handle anything. Scared of nothin'. Indestructible."

Without another word, Cody and Matt drift away in the general direction of Matt's old Ford pickup.

Shane lingers a little longer.

Tommy makes eye contact with him and gives him an *I'm serious* expression.

"Yes, sir," he says. "I always am. I always do. I will. Love you."

"Love you," Tommy says.

"Love you too," Johanna says.

The sweet sentiment coming from her soft little voice beneath her big, brown, kind eyes melts my heart and makes me want to envelop her in hugs and kisses.

As if somehow having a premonition of the import of this particular parting, Shane hesitates another moment before leaving.

"Love y'all," he says, then turns and slowly drifts away, disappearing into the crowd of people moving about.

Chapter Two

"What is it?" Tommy asks.

"Huh?" I say.

"What are you looking at?"

"Oh. I thought I saw Megan over there in the crowd, but I can't be sure."

"Why the look?"

"I'm sure it's nothing," I say. "Just looked like she was over there watching Shane from a distance and then started following him."

"Let me call him," Tommy says, pulling his phone from his pocket. "I hope word hasn't gotten back to her. She's a sweet person and has been a good girlfriend. She's gonna be hurt as it is. I don't want it to be worse than it has to be."

"Breakups are so difficult," Michelle says.

"That's why we don't ever intend to have one," Anna says, looking over at me.

"Exactly," I say, and kiss her on the head.

"Us either," Michelle says.

Tommy taps his phone and places it to his ear.

"Hey," he says after a moment, then starts smiling.

"Yeah, I miss you already. Hey, John thought he saw Megan. Is she with you? Well, look around. See if you see her. Is she supposed to be up here? Okay. Huh? Maybe so. I really think you should talk to her before you do anything else. Well, okay. It's your call, but think about it. And be careful down there. I'm serious. Yeah. Okay. Love you. Bye."

"What'd he say?" Michelle asks.

"Says he hasn't seen her and she's supposed to be in Panama City with her sister."

Since Wewa is such a small town and Panama City is so close, many locals do most of their shopping, eating out, and entertainment activities in the larger city just a thirty minute drive away.

"I could've sworn that it was her," I say, "but . . ."

"Eyes aren't what they used to be," he says.

"Nothing is."

"I wouldn't say that," Anna says with a sweet, sexy smile.

"This has been a long time coming," Anna says.

We are walking hand in hand through the park, passing booths and stands and people, Tommy and Michelle each holding one of our daughters, close by, ambling about at their own pace.

"What's that?" I ask.

"This. Us. Our family."

"Way too long," I say.

"But we got here eventually."

"Yes we did," I say. "And I will never, ever take it for granted."

26

"What is it?" she asks.

"What is what?"

"Something passed behind your eyes. It was subtle and quick, but it was there. Pain? Sadness? What?"

"Just wish we had Johanna all the time."

"Me too. Maybe we will one day."

"Can't imagine her mother going for anything like that."

"It'll work out," she says. "Look how everything else has."

"Hard to argue with that," I say.

While Michelle holds Taylor and Tommy pushes Johanna on one of the swings, Anna and I step over to Reggie and Merrick's booth.

"How's it going?" I ask.

"We've almost sold out," Merrick says.

"Well, let us get some before you do," Anna says. "Do you have a two-pound jar left?"

"We already have yours set aside," Reggie says.

Her seventeen-year-old son, Rain, normally a friendly and outgoing kid, sits in the back of the booth on his phone, sullen and downcast.

Reggie notices me looking at him. "Girl problems," she says.

"Are there any other kind?" I say.

Merrick smiles knowingly.

"Sweet girl he was seeing," Reggie says. "At least, I thought she was. Didn't seem sketchy at all. But she ghosted him. Then after a week of not answering her phone, he finally gets through and it's her new boyfriend."

"Wow," I say. "That's tough."

"Keep trying to get him to let go and move on, but .
. . guess he's just not ready yet."

"You know I can hear you, right?" Rain asks, standing and walking to the front of the booth to stand beside
his mother. "I know you don't believe me, but I know she
wouldn't do it."

"What?" Reggie asks.

"Any of it. It's just not her. Know what I'm sayin'?
She ain't like that. Somethin's going on. Know what I'm
sayin'? Not gonna stop until I figure out what it is."

I nod.

"Look at that face," he says, holding his phone out
toward us.

He fingers through pictures of him with a pretty,
sweet-faced blonde girl at the beach, a ballgame, the carnival, and in the woods at a bonfire.

"Let me know if you want help looking into it," I
say.

"Thanks, but it's something I need to do on my own.
Know what I'm sayin'?"

I nod.

"Yeah, I offered to help him," Reggie says. "To put
the full force of the sheriff's department behind finding
out what—"

"Somebody change the subject," Rain says. "Please."

"I will," Anna says, looking over at Merrick. "We
want the honey and a subscription to the paper too."

"Just fill out this form," Merrick says.

As Anna fills out the form, I pull out my wallet.

"What's the damage for both?" I ask.

"On the house. Welcome to Wewa."

"We can't do that," I say. "We know how difficult it is to have a business in a small town."

"We insist," he says. "We're just glad you're here."

As I begin to thank him, my phone vibrates in my pocket.

It's Susan—my ex and Johanna's mom.

"Thank them some more while I take this," I say to Anna.

I then step over a few feet and answer the call, my pulse quickening a bit as I do.

I never know how things will go with Susan, never know what sort of mood she'll be in, which iteration of her I'll get.

Following our second split and our final divorce, she had refused to speak to me for nearly four years, and had hidden Johanna's very existence from me that entire time. I might still not know I had a daughter if I hadn't shown up at her parents' doorstep and discovered her for myself. Since then, everything between us has been tenuous, and I have attempted to keep her happy as much as possible in order to maximize my time with Johanna.

"Y'all still at the Tupelo Festival?" Susan asks.

"We are. Is everything okay?"

We aren't supposed to meet until tomorrow evening.

"I need to talk to you," she says. "I'll be there in a few minutes."

"Here?" I ask, unable to hide the surprise in my voice.

She lives some eighty miles away in Tallahassee and never comes here. Occasionally we meet, but most often I drive all the way over to pick up or deliver Johanna back.

"Yes, John," she says. "I'm coming into town now."

Chapter Three

"I'm glad you're finally part of Johanna's life," she says.

Her use of *finally* is disingenuous, since the only reason I wasn't part of Johanna's life from the moment she was born was because she had hidden her from me.

"I want to cry every time I think about missing the first few years," I say.

"I know in the long run it will be good for her."

I'm not sure what she means by that or why she'd even say it, but I learned long ago not to take the bait. She is fishing for a reaction. I am not going to give her one.

"That's what makes this so difficult," she says. "That and I know how you'll react."

"What're you talking about, Susan?" I say. "React to what?"

"Johanna and I are moving back to Atlanta."

"*What?*"

"It's time. I only moved to Tallahassee so Mom and Dad could help me with her while she was little. Now that she's older . . . it's time."

"No."

She nods. "Yes. I should've already done it. I've been dragging my feet. Why, I don't know exactly, but . . ."

"Why're you doing this?"

"It's my home. I need to be there. I've sacrificed so much—for you, then her. Now it's time for me to give myself a little something."

The lack of self-awareness or unmitigated denial contained in that one statement is astonishing. Essentially a self-centered and often selfish person, Susan has made little to no sacrifices for anybody over the course of her entire life.

"If you need time for you," I say, "to focus on yourself and take care of you, Johanna should live with us."

"*What? No.* Absolutely not."

"We could just reverse the arrangement we have now and—"

"No. We can't. I can't. I won't."

"We wouldn't even have to meet," I say. "I'll drive the entire way both ways—bringing her and picking her up."

"You'll drive six hours both ways twice a weekend every weekend?" she says.

"Yes."

"No. It's not about . . . It has nothing to do with that. She needs her mom."

"And her dad," I say.

"She needs her mother more."

"I don't think so," I say.

"Well, it's true. Regardless of what you might think, or try to convince yourself of."

"In our home she has two parents and a sibling who—"

"Anna is *not* her mother and never will be. *I'm* her mother. Me. No one else. I can't believe you'd say that

32

Anna is—"

"I didn't say Anna's her mother," I say. "I said she has two parents and a sibling. It's a good home for her. Would you at least consider letting her—"

"It's out of the question. We'll talk more about this later, figure out the details when you're not so emotional and irrational."

I start to say something but stop, refusing to take the bait.

"For now I just want to get her and go home," Susan says. "I've got a lot to do to get ready."

"What do you mean?" I ask.

"For the move. I have to—"

"No. What do you mean *get her*? We're supposed to meet tomorrow night. Why would you get her early—especially when you're saying you have so much to do?"

"I'm just afraid that . . . I'm concerned that now that you know, you might do something stupid."

"Like what?"

"Kidnap her or something."

"Are you serious?"

"John, don't forget we don't have a custody agreement."

"Sounds like we need one," I say.

"Perhaps we do, but for now we don't have one and you're only seeing her as much as you are because I'm being generous and thinking about what's best for my daughter. If you're going to act like this, I'm not sure being around you right now is what's best for her."

"Act like what? I'm not acting like anything. Given the circumstances, I'm being extremely—"

"I'm done," she says. "I can't deal with you when

33

you're like this."

"Are you okay?" Tommy asks.

I shake my head.

Susan is gone—and Johanna with her.

I have just returned from saying goodbye to her and am unable to hide how I'm feeling.

Anna, Michelle, and Tommy have been joined by Reggie and Merrick, and the five of them are sitting around a picnic table down by the lake. Taylor is asleep in her carrier on the table.

All around us the festival is fading, people packing up their booths, kids squeezing the last bit of fun out of their time on the ponies and the swings and playground equipment and in the bouncy castle.

"What was that about?" Anna asks. "Why'd she get her today instead of tomorrow?"

I tell her, not minding that the others hear.

"Oh, John," Anna says, standing and hugging me. "I'm so sorry. But we knew this was coming and we know what to do."

"I've never seen a daddy look at his little girl quite the way you do," Michelle says. "Why would she do this?"

"I'll tell you why," Anna says. "When John showed up at her door, she thought he was there for her. She introduced him to his daughter, who she had hidden from him for four years, and agreed to let him be a part of her life, thinking they were going to get back together. Things began to change when she found out we are together."

"You've been telling me we needed to get a custody agreement in place," I say.

34

"Good thing you're sleeping with an attorney," Tommy says.

"And not just any attorney," Anna says. "A great one. We've got to move fast, though. Did she mention when she plans to move?"

I shake my head.

"First thing Monday morning I'll file a petition for paternity," she says. "And for a temporary restraining order to keep her from moving until we can establish paternity and have a custody hearing—though they don't call it that any longer."

"Do you really think a judge will prevent her from moving?" I say.

"Hard to say. He or she is supposed to be guided by what's in the best interest for the child. It will depend on what reasons Susan gives for wanting to move back."

"Obviously, John being in her life is what's best for her," Tommy says.

"Take whatever time you need to for this," Reggie says.

"Thank you."

"What are his chances?" Merrick asks Anna.

"Hell, she named the child after him, his name is on the birth certificate as the father, and she's given him de facto visitation rights for the past six months or so. He's been paying far more child support than any court would require—and she's cashed every check. He'll get parenting rights. No question. Keeping her in the state . . . that's far more difficult."

Merrick nods.

No one says anything.

The weight of the situation resting heavily upon us.

The silence doesn't last long, though. Soon it's shattered by the ringing and vibrating of phone calls—three nearly simultaneously for me, Reggie, and Tommy.

Though the calls come from different people, the message of all three is the same. Something horrible has happened, and Shane is missing.

Chapter Four

While Michelle and Anna stay and help Rain dismantle Merrick's booth, Merrick, Reggie, Tommy, and I race toward the river. Merrick and Reggie in his car, Tommy and me in my unmarked Chevy Impala.

I have my department-issued .40 caliber Glock in a holster and my badge back on my belt—on the same side so people always see them together. The small-frame 9mm I normally wear in an ankle holster is locked in my gun safe at home, and I feel its absence.

"I could tell something just wasn't right," Tommy is saying, "I should have trusted my . . . gut."

As we round the curve just past Red Bull Island, the small white wooden crosses along the side of the road seem to glow in the late-afternoon sunlight in a way I've never noticed before.

"But I thought it had to do with his breaking up with Megan. I was so worried about her finding out before he did it or how it'd affect her that I . . . I didn't listen carefully enough."

I nod. I know what he means. I know how he feels. I have felt the same way before, but it's a lot of pressure to put on yourself—to feel responsible for your intuitions and their ability to warn.

Tommy breaks down and begins to cry.

I reach over and put my hand on his shoulder.

I slow as we reach the Dead Lakes. A man is fishing from the bridge, a bicycle propped against the cement railing beside him.

Formed when sandbars created by the Apalachicola River dammed the Chipola River, the Dead Lakes is a hauntingly beautiful cypress tree burial ground of nearly seven thousand acres.

On either side, rising out of the tannic waters, cypress trees and the jagged trunks of dead cypress trees make the area look like what it is. A flooded field full of dead trees.

Merrick is driving fast, his retro deep-water-blue Challenger hugging the curves of the winding Lake Grove Road like it has been designed to.

He loved the car the moment he first sat in it. Large. Classic. Muscular. Masculine.

He rarely gets to drive it like this and relishes the opportunity to open her up.

Beside him, in the passenger seat, Reggie is on the phone with the first deputy on the scene.

"Just stay there for now," she is saying. "Secure the area. Don't let anyone else launch right now. Search and rescue is on the way. Keep it clear for them . . . Okay. I'm five minutes out."

After disconnecting the call, she looks over at Merrick.

"It's okay to enjoy driving like this is a closed

38

course," she says, "but you might not want to look quite so happy about it."

The car actually comes off the ground as it hits the bump at the end of the bridge where it connects to the road.

"I've been thinking," he says. "I need a light and a siren to keep in here. One of those fireball teardrops to plug into the cigarette lighter and throw on the dash, or a light bar for the grill, or an LED for the visor."

"You've given this a lot of thought, haven't you?"

He smiles.

"That smile'll get you nearly anything," she says, "but . . ."

"But? But what?"

"I'm afraid you'd use it when I'm not around," she says. "You know . . . for when you just feel the need . . . the need for speed."

"Then maybe you should deputize me," he says.

She turns serious again. "I might need your help with this," she says. "Whatever it turns out to be."

Objects on either side of the car whir by in a bit of a blur.

On the driver's side, the swamp is thick and wet, the sunlight streaming through the tall trees barely bright enough to dapple the mud and cypress stumps below. On the passenger's side, small wooden homes and old single wide house trailers—both suspended on stilts to protect from floods—back up to the Chipola River.

"You got it," he says. "But things are different now. You have an entire department. And you've got John."

"I'd like to assign him to it but think he might be too distracted dealing with the custody of his daughter. Whatta you think?"

"I still think you should," he says. "He's good. And he's new—won't be swayed by the politics of it."

"See?" she says. "You're helping already."

"Besides, you know you and I will be working it anyway . . . so if he needs help or has to be away . . ."

"*You and I?*" she says.

"I may not be deputized yet, but I *am* an accredited member of the press and one hell of an investigative reporter."

"'One hell of an investigative reporter,'" she repeats. "That's not all you're one hell of. I remember a certain someone making me come twice before I even had my damn coffee this morning. Twice. Before my goddam coffee."

They are quiet a moment, thinking back fondly on this morning's entanglements, but then the landing comes into view and brings them out of their reverie.

"How many kids has the river taken from us?" she says.

"Too many."

A kid they had gone to school with, Ronald Raffield, a pudgy, freckle-faced boy everyone called Red Face Raffield, had vanished beneath the dark waters of the Apalachicola and had never been see again. Not a single sign of him in twenty years.

"God, I hope this isn't another one like Ronald," she says. "The only thing worse than the river taking your child is it taking him and never returning him. Never returning any part of him."

"Oh, God, John," Tommy is saying. "I don't think I can deal with this. You know what the river does. It takes our kids and it doesn't give them back."

I don't say anything. What is there to say? I just pat his shoulder.

I want to tell him that we don't know anything yet, that it is too soon to worry, that he is borrowing trouble from the future, that he should stay in this present moment for now—but it won't help, and it isn't true, and I'm not going to say something I don't believe.

"Please God, please, let him be alive," Tommy prays. "Please. I'm begging you. I've always done my best to serve you and I've never asked for much. Well, I'm asking now. Please let Shane be okay."

Silently, for his sake as much as Shane's, I join him in the same petition.

He continues to pray as we speed past the camps and cabins that back up to the Chipola River, past the low-lying swamp area, past the entrance to Iola Landing and Byrd Parker Road.

Gaskin Park, the small landing and boat launch where Lake Grove Road ends in the Apalachicola River, is mostly empty. No children on the playground equipment and swings. No families cooking out or under the old cement picnic pavilion. No one launching a boat or leaving with one. A handful of trucks and empty boat trailers are parked about, but we don't see a single soul except the deputy securing the scene until we pull up and park near the dock.

Only then is anyone visible—Cody, Matt, Megan, and an enormous kid I don't recognize.

41

The distance from where we park down to the surface of the water is some twelve feet or so.

Because the rise and fall of the river fluctuates so much, the dock is constructed in two parts—a platform up top at land level and a floating dock down in the water below, with an aluminum gangplank connecting them. As soon as I pull up, Tommy jumps from the car and runs across the landing and down the dock, his footfalls pounding heavily on the wood slats then clanging just as heavily on the aluminum gangplank.

"WHERE?" he yells at the kids. "WHERE IS HE?"

They point to a place about fifteen feet out from the dock.

"WAIT," the deputy yells.

Without stopping or even slowing, Tommy dives into the green-tinged water, rippling the surface of the river, disappearing below.

Chapter Five

"What happened?" I ask the kids.

The four of them are huddled up near the entrance of the dock not far from the picnic pavilion. Matt and Cody are in blue jeans cutoffs. No shirts. No shoes. No towels. Their bodies, including their hair, appear to be completely dry. Megan is in an American flag bikini, a partially unzipped life vest clinging to her small, narrow body. The other kid, the one I don't recognize, is a huge black kid in knee-length swimming trunks, an enormous wet T-shirt plastered to his big body.

"We were getting ready to leave," Matt says. "We'd all just been in there together. Swimming. I reached the car and looked around. Cody was coming up. There was no sign of Shane. I was like, 'Where the hell is Shane?'"

"I's just walkin' up," the ginormous kid says. "I wasn't with them. I's swimmin' when they got here and I'a swim whenever and wherever I want to, so I stayed. I'd been to the bathroom over there, then got a snack out my car. I's walkin' back up when they started talkin' about where is Shane."

I nod. "And you are . . ."

"Swolle."

"Swolle?"

"'Cause he's all swolle up," Cody says. "Always has been."

"Not your nickname," I say.

"Daronté," he says. "Daronté Jackson."

I turn and look at Megan. "Where were you?"

She doesn't respond.

"Megan."

Appearing to be in shock, she just stares down at the river, water dripping from her hair. Her skin is pale and clammy and she's shaking.

I grab her shoulders and give her a little shake.

Her eyes close for a moment. When she reopens them, she looks at me.

"Megan."

"Yeah."

"Where were you when all this happened?"

"Coming in over there," she says, jerking her head toward the boat ramp. "I had just driven up on my Jet Ski."

Tommy breaks the surface of the water, reaching out and grabbing the dock with his hand, takes several deep breaths, and pushes himself back under.

"At first I figured that's where he was," Cody says. "Figured he hopped on the back with Megan again. Didn't know where else he could be. We didn't even start looking for him right away."

"But when we saw Megan walking up alone . . ." Matt says.

The first search and rescue boat arrives, and the diver wastes no time backing the boat down into the water and launching it.

In another moment, Merrick and Reggie arrive, the

retro Challenger locking up and screeching to a stop back by the patrol car about fifty feet from where we are near the dock.

"How long has it been?" I say.

"Since we first noticed he was missing?" Matt asks. "I'd say fifteen minutes. Maybe. Not long."

"We called right away," Cody says.

"How long was it between the last time you saw him and when you noticed he was missing?"

Matt and Cody look at each other. Megan just continues to gaze out at the water.

They both shrug.

Finally, Matt says, "Couldn't've been too long. Couple of minutes. Maybe. Maybe a minute. Not sure."

"What is it, Megan?" I say.

She doesn't respond.

"Megan."

"Huh?" she says, attempting to focus her attention onto me.

"What is it?" I say again.

She shakes her head as tears begin to stream down her cheeks.

"What happened?" I say. "It's okay. Just tell me what happened."

"What did you do to him?" Cody says.

Her face clouds up and she looks confused and agitated, as if asked a question she should know the answer to but doesn't.

"Yeah," Matt says. "You were out there near him, then he's gone."

I realize it's been a while since Tommy has come up for air.

Yelling for Reggie, I wave her over, then turn to look back at the water again.

Reggie, Merrick, and the deputy run up as the search and rescue boat speeds out of the landing and into the river, heading downstream.

"Will you two stay with them for a moment?" I say to Merrick and the deputy.

Taking Reggie by the arm, I lead her out of earshot of the kids.

"They need to be separated and we need to get statements from them," I say. "We need to thoroughly search their belongings and vehicles too. Charm them. Manipulate them. Get them to think they're helping you."

"I'll take them to the substation," she says. "They'll never know what hit 'em. I'm assuming you'll explain later."

"I will, but Tommy's in the water. I need to go down and check on him. Megan might be going into shock or she might be faking. She seems to know something or needs to say something. The boys say she was near Shane on her Jet Ski before he disappeared."

"I got it," she says. "Go."

I run over to the dock and rush down the gangplank, pulling my wallet, keys, and phone out as I do.

Reaching the bottom floating platform, I kick off my shoes and begin to place the items from my pockets in them, but before I finish, Tommy pops up out of the water, gasping for air.

I move over to where he is.

"I was just about to come in after you," I say.

"I can't see anything down there," he says. "I'm just feeling around."

"Come on, let me help you out," I say, reaching

down and extending him a hand.

He shakes his head, wiping water from his eyes and pushing the matted wet hair from his forehead.

"I can't stop," he says. "Not until I find him."

Soon, he'll be in the way of search and rescue and we'll have to force him out of the water, but for now, I understand what he's doing and why and why he can't stop, why he won't until we force him to.

"Okay," I say, "but come back up more often. Won't help anyone if you drown."

Chapter Six

"**Y**'all know I'm new, right?" Reggie says to the group of kids. "My name is Reggie. And not only am I a girl—the first ever to be sheriff in Gulf County—but I wasn't even elected. The governor appointed me. I'm doing my best to do a good job, but it's not easy. I don't really have a lot of experience and everybody's watching me. Everybody wants me to fail."

The three young men nod, and seem somewhat sympathetic.

Megan continues to shake and stare off into the distance.

"So I could really use y'alls help. And I'd really appreciate it. I just need to do everything by the book, follow proper procedures and prove to everyone that a girl can do this job, you know?"

More nods.

"But I also want y'all to be comfortable and get this over with as quick as possible. I know y'all are worried about your friend. So let's do this, can we? Let's go uptown to the substation and let's get your statements and let you go, okay?"

They nod again.

"It's just standard procedure, but we need to do a quick search of your vehicles . . . And I certainly don't want y'all to have to ride to town in the back of a patrol car. Tell you what, why don't we take a quick look in your cars and then y'all just drive up to the substation and I'll meet you there?"

"Sounds good to us," Cody says.

Matt nods.

She looks over at Swolle.

"Fine with me."

"Just help me remember to get y'all to sign a consent form and a Miranda warning form, will you? Last one of these I did, I forgot to get one. Felt like such a fool. So embarrassing."

"No problem," Matt says. "We'll remind you."

"Thanks. And as soon as I hear anything about Shane, I'll let y'all know."

"Cool," Cody says.

"Sweetheart, are you all right?" Reggie asks Megan.

Megan doesn't respond.

"Come on," Reggie says. "She can ride with me. Let's get up there and get her dry and warm and make sure she's okay."

"Shit, don't treat her too good," Matt says. "She probably killed Shane."

Other search and rescue boats arrive and are launched.

The original deputy securing the scene is replaced by another.

Gawkers, onlookers, and just the mildly curious begin to show up, all of them turned away by the deputy before they can even enter the landing.

A mobile command center unit is brought in and set up, and one of the members of search and rescue pulls up in his enormous RV and proceeds to set up a camp of sorts. Soon beneath its awning and in an E-Z-Go popup tent beside it there are chairs and tables, carafes of coffee, bottles of water, and an assortment of snacks.

Eventually another member arrives with a large cooker and begins to grill hamburgers, hotdogs, and chicken patties.

And the late-afternoon sun continues to get lower and lower in the clear May sky.

As I stand on the dock, keeping an eye on Tommy, I look out over the wide, winding river. Search and rescue boats move about, mostly along the banks, ripples from their wakes rocking the dock back and forth and up and down. Across the green-tinged waters, a small houseboat is moored to a tree on the other side. Beyond it, a thick, verdant river swamp of cypress and pine and oak ascends the hill, appearing impenetrable. Overhead a couple of swallow-tailed kites glide by, and down the way near the bank on this side, a great blue heron stalks its prey in the reedy shallows.

This time when Tommy breaks the surface of the water and grabs onto the dock, he lingers a little.

"I know what I'm doing is useless and futile at this point," he says. "I know I look like a ridiculous fool, but I've got to do something. I can't just . . ."

"I understand," I say. "I do. I'd be doing the same thing, but . . . it's time to let search and rescue take over now. They know what they're doing. They'll find him."

"I know how absurd it is, but I feel like if I get out

of the water, I'm giving up on him being alive. Like I'm admitting that he's gone. Really gone. I know he is. I know it's been too long for there to be any chance, but . . . I keep hoping I can find him and bring him up and give him CPR and he'll be fine. Or that he's trapped in an air bubble or something equally ludicrous, but . . ."

My heart breaks for him, and I blink back tears as I empty my pockets and take off my shirt and shoes so I can join him in his futile search for his brother who is more like a son.

Chapter Seven

Evening.

The setting sun behind us bathes the river before us and the treetops along the banks on the other side with a translucent golden glow so soft, so subtle, it's sublime.

The water is wide. The river is relentless.

The Apalachicola River runs over a hundred miles from the Georgia-Florida line to empty into the Apalachicola Bay. Along the way it feeds an enormous floodplain, gives life to verdant river swamp. The Chipola River, its main tributary and the sacred source of the Dead Lakes, flows into and out of and beside it for a not insignificant part of the way.

The stunning natural beauty of our surroundings and the quality of light illuminating and emphasizing its breathtaking brilliance causes a severe disconnect and cognitive dissonance that contrasts the real reason and grim realities of why we are here and what we're doing.

No one has verbalized it yet, but everyone knows it—even those who refuse to admit it to themselves. We are now looking for the drowned and lifeless body of Shane McMillan.

Four Wewa Search and Rescue boats are now in the

water. One is anchored in the middle of the river about three miles downstream. Two search the banks—one on each side. The last, equipped with a side-scan sonar, is thirty feet off the right side bank, working his way downriver, taking scans every fifteen feet or so.

Merrick, who lives less than a mile away on Byrd Parker Drive, has just taken Tommy to his house to get cleaned up and borrow a dry set of clothes.

I am standing on the dock with Reggie and Ralph Raffield. Ralph is the head of search and rescue and the older brother of Ronald Raffield, the still-missing boy whose disappearance led to the formation of Wewa Search and Rescue.

Ralph is dropping flotation devices with weights that hang down about eighteen inches on them into the water.

"This'll give us some indication of the surface flow," he says, "and show us where something might get hung up."

The *something* he's talking about is Shane's body, and we all know it, but I'm glad he uses *something*.

Reggie looks on with what she refers to as her "resting bitch face"—the default state of her face when she has no expression.

"It helps that we know approximately where he was when he went under," he adds.

His team, a group of well-trained and dedicated volunteers, had already spoken to the witnesses about Shane's general whereabouts, what he was wearing, and his description, including height and weight and hair color. They had also taken water temps and measured the current.

"We get all the information we can, but then it just comes down to a SWAG," he says.

I wait for Reggie to ask, but she doesn't have to.

"A scientific wild ass guess," he adds.

Now a small man in his midforties with red-tinged hair going gray, he had been twenty-five when his fifteen-year-old brother vanished beneath the surface of the Apalachicola never to resurface again. It's hard to fathom that Red Face Raffield, the pudgy, freckle-faced boy the river took and never returned, would be in his midthirties now.

"Since you two are new," Ralph says, "I'd like to go over a few things up front. Share my philosophy."

"Sure," Reggie says, nodding enthusiastically and giving him a small smile.

She is tired and tense with the pressure and responsibility and weight of this, but it doesn't take away from her rough natural beauty, her stunning—though at the moment squinting—eyes, and her skin that resembles riverbed clay in the evening sunlight.

"You're the boss and we work for you—under your authority, but we know what we're doing," he says. "I strongly suggest you take our recommendations."

"I know you do," she says. "And I will. You won't get any interference from me. I'm here to support your operation and give you anything you need."

"We work all over," he continues, as if he has a planned script he intends to finish, "have more equipment and experience and resources than all but the largest counties in the tristate region. We roll up on a place and get the job done. No matter what it takes. All over, people who've worked with us before call us 'high-tech rednecks,' and we wear it like a badge of honor."

"Which you should," Reggie says.

"Everything we do, we do for the families of the

victims," he says. "That's important. I've been there. I know how important that is. Firsthand. You know how long we'll stay at this? How long we'll keep searching? I'll tell you. Our philosophy is simple. We go home when the family does."

Reggie and I nod.

"Speaking of family," he says. "They're gonna want to be involved. I know Tommy has already been in the water. Well, I let them be. I've been right where Tommy is now. So I get it. You want to help. You want to do something—anything—to keep from going crazy. So I let them be involved. But . . . I don't think it's in their best interest to find the body, so . . . I usually let them do other things—out of the water. Like search the hill. Stuff like that."

The hill is what we in North Florida call the river banks, the swamps, and any land around the river.

Reggie nods. "I like that approach," she says.

"Cadaver dogs will be here a little later," he says. "Coming from Montgomery. We may find him before then, but if not, between the sonar scans and the dogs, we should locate him soon. If we don't, then we'll start dragging the bottom. The current is flowing pretty fast right now so . . . Think about it. How long has it been since he went under? An hour? More? If the river is only flowing a mile an hour, he could be a mile downstream by now. That's why we have the observation boat three miles down. If we don't find him soon, I'll move it even farther down. 'Course the river has so much stuff in it and there's so many exposed cypress root systems along the banks, a body usually gets hung up on something rather than just free flowing downstream. I've seen it both ways, though."

His radio sounds. It's Fred Hall, the man doing the

sonar scans. The first scans are complete and ready to be looked at.

Who helps the helper, Merrick thinks as he drives Tommy the short distance down Byrd Parker Drive to his house.

Byrd Parker Dive is a half-circle road winding around next to the Chipola River, beginning and ending in two different places on Lake Grove Road—one at the landing, one about a mile before it. It is lined on both sides with houses, river camps, rentals, and lots where houseboats are tied up.

In the seat beside him, Tommy is shaking, his long hair dripping down on his soaked shirt. He seems to notice neither.

"I wish I knew what to say," he says.

Tommy shakes his head. "Nothing to say."

"I was just thinking . . . you've helped so many people. You help so many people all the time. You're who they'd call in for something like this. I'm sure you know just what to say, but me . . . I'm at a loss. Sorry."

"You're doing all that can be done," Tommy says. "You're showing me kindness and concern. You're taking care of my immediate needs. You're here. That's what matters. That's all that matters."

He's right, Merrick thinks. When I lost Monica and Ty, my mom, my dad, nothing anyone said mattered. Nothing helped.

His mind goes back to the night of the accident. Monica bringing Ty back from a doctor's appointment. The rain. The hard, relentless rain. The wet roads. Low-lying area. Flooded. Hitting the water. Hydroplaning. Losing control. Flipping. Rolling. Crashing. Through the guardrail. Sinking into the Dead Lakes. Her dead from the impact but Ty . . . Ty . . .

"You just lost your dad," Tommy says. "I should be asking after you."

Merrick shakes his head. "No. Not at all."

He and his dad had been close—more at certain times in his life than others—but losing a parent, as difficult as it is . . . is natural, is . . . What was it Claudius said to Hamlet? He'd done his best to memorize it when he'd read it recently.

'Tis sweet and commendable in your nature, Hamlet,
To give these mourning duties to your father.
But you must know your father lost a father,
That father lost, lost his, and the survivor bound
In filial obligation for some term
To do obsequious sorrow. But to persever
In obstinate condolement is a course
Of impious stubbornness. 'Tis unmanly grief.

The father Merrick lost had himself lost a father, but a child, a child is another matter, another matter entirely.

His mind goes to the dark place again.

Monica unconscious, dead behind the wheel. Ty trapped in his car seat. The dark waters of the Dead Lakes rising around him.

When Merrick reaches his little clapboard house, he pulls into the yard, cuts the lights, kills the engine, but makes no move to get out.

Both our sons drowned, he thinks, killed by the same body of water.

Technically, Shane was Tommy's brother, but only technically. He was a son to him.

In the same way Casey and Kevin are my children, he thinks. The exact same way. They couldn't be any more my children if I were their biological father.

As if he has access to his thoughts, Tommy says, "You . . . you lost a son, didn't you?"

Merrick nods. Unable to speak.

Perhaps excessive mourning for a father is an unmanly grief, but there is no grief too extreme, too excessive, to expressive for the loss of a child. There is no loss like the loss of a child.

"Sorry," Tommy says. "I just . . . I'm just . . . grasping for . . ."

Overwhelmed. Overcome. Merrick breaks down and begins to sob.

Leaning over in the seat, Tommy breaks down too as he hugs him.

For a long moment, the two men, mere acquaintances, connected like few humans will ever be, sob uncontrollably, clinging to one another as they do.

Chapter Eight

The search and rescue command center is a mobile unit
brought in by EOS.

Reggie and I are inside it with Ralph and Kate, a
young woman with light brown hair in a ponytail above a
search and rescue windbreaker and shorts, looking at the
images from the sonar scans on a fifty-inch monitor.

"The moment PIW ingests water and goes down—"

"PIW?" Reggie asks.

"Person in water," he says. "When they sink—usually
at a forty-five-degree angle—they go down and stay down
until the gas in their body begins to be released and ex-
pands and they begin to float."

She nods.

"When the body first starts floating a bit it may
bounce along the bottom," he says. "It takes a while for the
body to rise all the way up and float—and sometimes they
never do. Can get hung up on something on the bottom
or along the bank. Sonar scans can show us what's down
there."

"How good an image can you get?" Reggie asks.

"You're about to see," he says. "Real good—though
not in dark river water. In a clear lake or spring or even a

bay we've been able to see facial features, scars, things like that. In water like this it may just look like a shadow or dark spot. As soon as Fred fills up an SD card or finishes a section, he sends it in so Kate here can look at the images while he continues to take them of other sections. Each image has GPS coordinates on it so if we get something we know where it is—or was at the time the image was taken. We'll send a cadaver dog into the area without telling its handler anything and see what he gets. The moment a person drowns, microscopic bubbles begin to rise from their body. You and I can't see them, but a well-trained dog can smell them. Once we get double confirmation like that, we'll send divers down."

As he is talking, we watch the screen as Kate carefully examines each image before going onto the next one.

"Wait," Reggie says, as Kate changes the image on the screen. "Go back. What is that?"

She points to a dark area near the bottom right side of the screen.

"Part of an old boat hull," she says. "Been there for as long as I can remember."

"Oh. Sorry."

"Don't be," Kate says. "I can miss stuff. And I have a tendency to go too fast, so always speak up if you think you see something."

"The river is full of stuff," Ralph says. "All kinds of old objects and debris. Even bodies the dogs will sometimes alert on."

Reggie and I both shoot him looks.

"Ancient bodies," he says. "Indians. Homesteaders. People buried along the banks of the river who are now in it because the river has shifted over the past hundred years."

We both nod.

Kate continues to move through the images at a pretty fast clip.

"If none of this turns up anything," Ralph says, "we'll start dragging the river in the morning."

"**I**'d like you to head this up," Reggie says.

The two of us are standing on the landing, away from everyone else.

Out in the river, the search and rescue boats move about, up and down the river along the banks, in the last of the light.

I nod.

"Because of the nature of it, I'll stay involved, but it'll be your case," she says. "It's most likely just an accidental drowning, but . . . we'll do a thorough investigation to be sure."

"Some things already don't add up," I say. "With the kids. Do we have statements from them?"

She nods.

"Who interviewed them?"

"Me, Walt, and Denny," she says. "So . . . should be good."

"I'll read their statements. Listen to their interviews and then do a follow-up tomorrow."

I am scheduled to work at the prison tomorrow, and will have to go in for a while, but will only do what I absolutely have to so I can focus on what needs to be done in the investigation.

"I know you know what you're doing," she says, "but

61

tread lightly. Remind them of their Miranda. Find the truth but remember they're kids."

"Kids can be killers," I say. "But I'd call them young adults."

"Too true," she says. "Do what you've got to, but . . . be wise. What's not adding up?"

"May be nothing, but . . . I have questions about the statements they first gave me when I got here. That's why I wanted them separated and to give individual statements and be interviewed separately and on the record. I'll know more after I read and listen to what they said."

"That's not much."

"Their appearance didn't match their statements," I say.

"Whatta you mean?"

"The boys, who said they just got out of the water, were dry, and the girl, who was supposed to have been on a Jet Ski, was wet."

"Really?"

"And the big guy, the one they call Swolle, he said something . . . something like he had a right to swim here too. Like maybe they had words or something."

"You thinkin' racial?"

"Maybe. We'll see."

"Anything else?" she asks.

"Yeah, there was nothing with them or on the dock. No clothes, no shoes, no coolers, no towels, no phones, no speakers. Nothing. If they had alcohol or drugs, I get wanting to hide them before we got here, but to take the time to put everything up when you think your friend is drowning . . ."

"Shane could've been on something that contributed to him drowning," she says.

I nod. "It's why we have to treat this entire area as a crime scene and we need to search it as soon as we can. Treat it like a crime scene, and if it turns out to be an accidental drowning, we're in good shape. Treat it only like a search and rescue scene of an accidental drowning, and if it turns out to be a homicide, we'll lose evidence we need to build our case."

"God, I'm glad we have you, John," she says. "So glad."

Chapter Nine

Night.

It's full dark now, and the search continues beneath banks of halogen lights brought in and set up near the guardrail.

Most point down toward the river, but a few are aimed at the area around the RV and mobile command center.

The entire landing is lit like a high school football field, the illumination dropping off fast at the edges, the night appearing even darker than it normally would because of the contrast.

The search and rescue boats are also equipped with lamps that light up the area around them as well as handheld Q-Beams for flooding a particular spot.

"Think we'll find him?" Reggie asks.

"Thought they would have already," I say.

"I'm really beginning to wonder if we will."

As Merrick and Tommy arrive back at the landing from Byrd Parker Drive, I see Anna and Michelle pulling up from

Lake Grove Road.

Merrick pulls over and parks close to us.

Anna is stopped by the deputy stationed at the entrance to the landing.

"Will you radio Bartholomew and tell her to let Anna and Michelle through?" I ask Reggie.

She does.

When Merrick and Tommy walk up I can see that both men have been crying. Bloodshot eyes. Still damp. Sniffling occasionally. And I have a whole new appreciation for Merrick.

I step over and hug Tommy.

He hugs me back, holding on tightly for a long moment.

When we release each other, I do the same to Merrick.

Reggie looks over at us, a bemused look on her face.

"That's what you get when you hire a chaplain to be one of your investigators," Merrick says.

"I guess it is."

Anna and Michelle park, get out, and rush over to us, Michelle and Tommy breaking down as they embrace.

Anna hugs me and asks, "How're you holdin' up?"

"Y'all're some huggin' folks," Reggie says loud enough for us but not Tommy and Michelle to hear.

I nod. "I'm okay. How are you? Where's Taylor?"

"She's asleep in her bed. Aunt C is there listening out for her. I'm not gonna stay long, but I had to see you. And I told Michelle I'd bring her."

"I'm glad you did," I say. "You feel so good."

"I know you've got a lot going on, but don't forget to call Johanna and tell her good-night."

"I was just about to when you pulled up. What time is it?"

I walk several feet away to make the call.

"I'm not going to argue with you anymore tonight," Susan says as she answers the phone.

"I just called to say good-night to Johanna," I say.

"Oh," she says, disappointment in her voice. "Well, okay then. Hold on."

When Susan puts her on the phone, I sing to her, as I often do, the first line of the old Kool and the Gang song.

"Johanna . . . I . . . love you."

"Hey Daddy."

Her soft, sweet voice is also sleepy, making it even more airy.

"I miss you," I say.

"I miss you, Daddy."

"What're you up to?"

"Nothin'."

"Nothing at all?"

"Havin' a snack before bed."

"Is it good?"

"No, not really."

"I'm sorry."

"It's okay, Daddy. What are you doing?"

"Just missing my girl. Wishing you were still here. I love you so much."

"I love you."

"Sleep well and have sweet dreams," I say. "I'll talk to you tomorrow."

"You too, Daddy. Night night."

When I return to the others, they are trying to talk Tommy into going home.

"I just can't," he says. "I know I'm not helping anything by being here, but it helps me."

Anna turns to me. "Sheriff says for me to make you go home," she says.

I shake my head. "I—"

"It wasn't a suggestion," Reggie says.

"But I—"

"You're in charge of the investigation," she says, "not search and rescue. Get some rest so you'll be fresh to conduct the interviews tomorrow. That's what matters. That's what's important."

"She's right," Anna says.

I begin to nod very slowly. "Okay."

Chapter Ten

"**I** can't believe he's gone," Tommy is saying.

He finally relented and agreed to go home for a little while. I am driving him and Michelle home while Anna heads directly to our house to relieve her aunt so it'll be just the two of us when I get there.

"Doesn't seem real," he adds.

"Can't imagine it ever will," Michelle says.

"I wish he would've stayed in Fort Benning instead of coming home this weekend," Tommy says. "Would he still be alive if he had, or was it just his time and he'd've been taken no matter where he was?"

I don't say anything, just listen.

"Whatta you think, John?" Michelle asks.

"Yeah," Tommy says, "I was really asking. Do you think we all have a certain number of days, and the day and hour of our death is already determined, or do we have some say in the matter?"

"I think we have some say."

"So if he wouldn't've come home this weekend . . . or if I had said no when he asked for permission to go to the landing . . ."

"There's no way to know for sure," I say, "and you

can drive yourself crazy second-guessing yourself and your decisions. I've done it plenty of times before."

"I believe God ordains it," Michelle says. "I don't think it's up to us. Only to him."

I get the appeal of that kind of thinking, the simplicity and irresponsibility of believing or wanting to believe that everything happens for a reason, that it is just God's will, that we have no autonomy, agency, or responsibility, but I think it's naive wishful thinking that doesn't take into account the entirety of the evidence and the state of the world. Is this world a place where only God's will is done?

"What do you think?" Michelle asks Tommy.

He shakes his head. "Right now I don't know what to think about anything. Not anything at all."

We ride in silence for a few moments, moonlight edifying the tall tips of pines on either side of the car.

"Is there even a chance it wasn't just an accident?" Tommy asks.

"Why do you—"

"I overheard some of the deputies and search and rescue people talking. They seem to suspect Megan."

Michelle gulps in a sudden intake of air. "Oh my God."

"I honestly don't know," I say. "I've been charged with finding out. My investigation starts tomorrow."

"I just can't see her doing anything like that," Tommy says. "Not under any circumstances."

"I can't believe it's already being talked about," Michelle says.

"Be careful with her, John," Tommy says. "Take care of her no matter what happened."

"I will," I say. "An accident is still the most likely

scenario."

By the time I get home, Anna is waiting for me on our back patio.

She is sitting on one of the two wooden Adirondack chairs, a glass of wine in one hand and a baby monitor in the other, looking out at the lake.

Julia is tranquil tonight, picture-still beneath the pale, partial moon, the cypress trees in the foreground so stately and staid as to appear part of a painting.

I lean over and kiss her, touching her face and taking my time, before sitting in the chair beside her.

She hands me a frosted stein of the triple-berry fruit smoothie I like so much, and we clink glasses and say "Cheers."

"To true love," I say.

I'm exhausted, but I have so many thoughts darting around inside my skull I'm not ready for bed yet.

We sit in silence for a long moment, looking out at Julia, at the moonlight shimmering on her black glass surface, taking in the peace and beauty like sacraments.

"How are you?" she asks.

"I'm okay. Depleted, but . . ."

"We'll do what we have to to be a big part of Johanna's life," she says. "I know we just moved and I love it here, but if we have to move to Atlanta, we will."

Tears sting my aching eyes. "The perfect thing to say. Thank you. You're perfect."

"What Tommy and Michelle are going through is a reminder of what really matters most in this life," she says.

I nod.

We fall silent again, each taking a sip from our drink.

"Any reason to think it wasn't an accident?" she asks.

"A few. Maybe. I'll know more tomorrow when I interview the kids who were with him."

"Thought you had to be at the prison tomorrow?"

"I do."

"Well," she says, standing, "we need to get you to bed."

"Won't be able to sleep."

"Will when I get through with you."

That night I dream of drowning.

I know from what I've studied and the crime scenes I've seen that drowning is a particularly unpleasant way to die.

Lungs filling with water, losing their ability to transfer oxygen into the bloodstream.

Struggling to breathe, forcing water into the sinuses.

Coughing. Triggering the inhalation reflex. Pulling even more water into the lungs.

Loss of air and exertion from struggle cause oxygen levels in the blood to plummet rapidly.

Loss of consciousness.

Loss of heartbeat.

Loss of life.

Chapter Eleven

"You're a cop?" Will asks.

He's a gentle, young black man with dark skin and a gap between his two front teeth. He's intelligent and insightful and has a wisdom beyond his years. In the short time I have been here, I've witnessed his integrity and leadership. He's respected by both the inmates and the staff.

We're in my office in the chapel of the Gulf Correctional Institution on Sunday morning following the interfaith service.

"Just wanted to ask before we got started," he says. "I heard you weren't just our chaplain, but a cop too."

"Who told you that?" I ask.

"It's all over the compound. You know how this place is."

I nod. A lot like a small town—only worse.

He's assigned to Laundry, and his inmate uniform is neat and pressed and fits him well.

"So is it true?" he says. "It's just you don't seem like a cop."

Though he's assigned to Laundry, he spends a lot of time volunteering in the chapel, using the library, taking classes, helping out the inmate clerks assigned here.

"I'm an investigator with the sheriff's department," I say. "And I'm a chaplain."

"Isn't that some sort of conflict of interest?" he says.

I shake my head. "No. Why would you think so?"

"How can we trust you?" he says. "How can we tell you anything? Confess anything to you?"

"You can tell me anything and it will be kept in the strictest of confidence—except a crime or your intention to commit one, or that you plan to hurt yourself or others. And that's true of all counselors."

He doesn't say anything.

"I've been a minister *and* an investigator my entire adult life," I say. "I've always done both."

"But . . ."

"What?" I ask.

"You're a cop," he says. "A . . . cop. How can you expect to . . . do . . . any good in here. Cops are our enemies. They're corrupt. Racist. Abusive."

"I'm not," I say. "I'm not any of those things."

"But that's our experience, that's our perception. Cops kill us with impunity."

I nod. He's right about the perception, about the lines that have been drawn on the streets, and I can't believe it didn't occur to me.

We are quiet a long moment.

Finally, he says, "Is there another chaplain I can talk to?"

As I'm leaving GCI for the day, feeling down and defeated, I am stopped by Vicki Healey, a short, dumpy forty-something correctional officer with very high eyebrows and an even higher opinion of her importance to the community.

"Hey, John, right? I'm Vicki with an *i* Healey. My husband, Norman, is a city commissioner."

I nod and extend my hand. "Nice to meet you."

"I hear you're investigating the disappearance of that poor Shane McMillan."

I nod again.

Vicki with an *i* has a reputation of inserting herself into issues and events and situations that have nothing to do with her and would be far better if she left it that way. She and her daughter are perpetually on social media and run a number of Facebook groups, ostensibly for selling and trading items and notifying citizens of upcoming events in the community, but actually used for spreading gossip and manufacturing drama more than anything else.

"You may not know, but my Kimmy and I run a number of community service–related Facebook groups."

"I've heard."

"We're on social media a lot and really have a sense of where the community is in its thinking, and the pulse of the town points to that Megan Stripling having something to do with Shane's disappearance. Did you see what she posted on her page last night?"

"No."

"Read like a confession to me. My Kimmy goes to school with her and says she's always been sort of sad and disturbed. Anyway, she tried to post on a couple of our Wewa pages, but we wouldn't let her."

"What was she trying to post?"

"Asking for prayers and support and for everyone downstream to keep an eye out for Shane's body."

"And why didn't you let her post that?"

"Because she's just trying to get sympathy. She's playin' people—some of the same people who could be on a jury if she's arrested."

"Right now all we have is a missing young man in what appears to be an accidental drowning," I say. "Megan is no more a suspect than you are. Less so after this conversation."

"Wait. *What?*"

Chapter Twelve

I call Anna on my way to the substation.

"Hello handsome," she says.

"How's my girl?"

"Working hard to get your other girl back," she says. "I'll have everything ready to file first thing in the morning."

"Thank you so much. I can't tell you how much I appreciate you."

"Maybe not, but you could try showing me later tonight when you get home."

"Count on it," I say. "How's our other girl?"

"Taking a nap. Full and happy prior to that."

I remove my clerical collar as I drive, transitioning from one role to another, the act itself helping me with a shift in mindset.

Part of the reason I am working two jobs is so I can afford to give Susan far more child support than any judge would order and so that Anna can take her time in healing and raising Taylor. But that's only part of it. The truth is, I've always done both jobs, have always been a cop who ministers or a minister who investigates. Now I actually get paid for both.

"I got another collect call from Chris today."

Chris is her soon-to-be ex-husband, an attorney awaiting trial in Tallahassee.

"Did you accept?"

"No. Don't plan to. Ever. We know what he wants."

Yes, we do. For her not to divorce him and for her to come to see him and bring Taylor when she does.

"Sorry. You okay?"

"I'm fine. Just a collect call. All I have to do is hang up."

He's Taylor's biological father and a judge has granted him visitation rights, which means we have to take her to the Leon County Jail twice a month, but that's all we're going to do—no matter how much he begs and pleads.

"Do you want to change your number?" I ask. "Or we can swap."

"That's sweet. I like the idea of him calling you."

"Then let's do that."

"We'll see," she says. "It probably won't be necessary, but thank you. Any word from Reggie?"

"Still searching. Haven't turned up anything yet."

"I sure was hoping they would have found him by now. It's horrific enough already. Not having his body is just . . ."

"Yes, it is."

We are quiet a moment and I can hear her breathing.

"You headed to conduct the interviews?"

"I am. Can I get you to do me a favor related to that?"

"Sure."

"Can you search social media, especially Facebook, to see what all Megan has posted?"

"Of course."

"Busybody Vicki with an *i* said she all but confessed."

"Which means nothing."

"No doubt, but I'd like to know what she posted. The boys too."

"You got it," she says. "What was Swolle's actual name again?"

"Daronté Jackson."

Daronté Jackson makes the seat he's sitting on look like a child's chair, as if we're in a pre-K classroom instead of the sheriff's substation office we use for interviews.

Since the sheriff's department is on the other end of Gulf County in Port St. Joe, we have a substation here in Wewa on Main Street close to the library and the old courthouse. It's in a small building that was once a pizza place and a doughnut shop and had started its life as a service station.

Everything about Swolle is enormous. Even seated he looks taller than most people do standing.

"Why we gotta do this two times?" he says.

While I'm interviewing him in the back office, I have a deputy in the outer office with the other two—preventing them from talking to one another, keeping them here so I can go back and forth between them if I need to.

"Maybe more than two before we're done," I say.

He cocks his huge head back and considers me. "Oh. Do it as many times as it takes to pin it on the black guy. That it?"

"You really think that's what we're trying to do?" I

say.

"Ain't like it ain't been done before."

"True," I say. "But that's not what's happening here. That's not something I would ever let happen. Ever. Everything you said before, everything you say today, is being recorded. Everything I say too. No one's trying to jam you up or make you ride the rap for somebody else. I'm not trying to coerce you or trick you. I'm just trying to understand what really happened. That's it. When we finish, I'll give you copies of the interviews we've done with you so you'll have your own record. Cool?"

He nods. "Ask away."

"You were in the water already when the three other guys arrived?"

He shrugs his massive shoulders. "'Pends on what you mean. I's sittin' on the dock with my legs down in the water. I don't really get all the way in the water."

"Was anyone else there?" I ask. "On the dock or in the water?"

He shakes his head. "Just me. And I's gettin' ready to leave when those fools showed up."

"But you didn't," I say. "Why not? What changed?"

"Just decided to stay."

"Why?"

"It's a free country."

"Is it?" I ask.

"It's supposed to be."

"Did they tell you to leave, indicate you should? Is that why you stayed?"

"They just sort of . . . They came in and took over. They large and loud and act like they own the place. Blasting music. Splashing around. Rocking the dock. Sayin' all kinda stupid ignorant-ass shit. My big black ass wasn't about to leave then. I get so sick of that shit, you know?"

I nod. "I do, and I'm sorry. So what happened?"

"Same shit that always happens. They act like I'm not there, like they own the world. Divin' off the dock, splashing water up on me and my phone. Never a *my bad* or *sorry* or nothin'."

"How'd things seem between them?"

"Fine, I reckon. I don't know, a little . . . like tense, maybe—'specially between Cody and Shane, but I could be wrong. That could be some shit I'm readin' into it."

"It was just the three guys?" I ask. "When did Megan arrive?"

"That's when shit really got retarded. I can't remember how long they's there before she pulled up on her little Jet Ski, but it wasn't too long."

"She didn't pull the Jet Ski to the landing on a trailer and unload it?" I ask.

He shakes his huge head. "She come up from the river, you know, like from upstream. Just drove right up on 'em. None of 'em happy to see her."

"Then what happened?"

"Then they took stupid to a whole new level."

"How?"

Chapter Thirteen

"Cody and Shane have always had this sort of competition going," Matt says. "But it's on steroids since Shane became a Ranger."

Soft and pale and flabby, Matt is good-natured and easygoing—not someone either Shane or Cody would feel the need to compete with.

"I think Cody kinda feels left behind," he continues. "He was the better athlete in school. The more popular kid. And he thought he was gonna be like this big baseball star—in college and then the major league, but he got cut from the college team that signed him and . . . he dropped out of college in the first semester, moved back home, and is basically doing nothing. So any chance to beat Shane at something. Anything."

"So they decide to race across the river," I say.

"Yeah. Swim across, fighting the current, dodging debris and boats and gators, touch the houseboat, and swim back. Whoever touched the dock first won."

It was a stupid, immature, impetuous thing to do. The river is extremely wide there. I'd guess two hundred yards. It'd be an exhausting swim even in the best of circumstances, but between the current and boat traffic and air pockets, tree limbs, snakes, turtles, and gators, it was testosterone-induced insanity.

"Whose idea was it?" I ask.

He narrows his eyes and tilts his head, seeming an attempt at accessing the memory. Eventually he begins to slowly shake his head. "I'm not sure I heard. Didn't really know about it until they were doing it."

"Who won?"

"Shane. He rubbed it in too."

"And this was after Megan showed up?" I ask.

"I think she's the real reason they did it. Showing off for her. Cody's always had a thing for her. And with her and Shane breaking up . . . it wouldn't've be long before he was . . . making his move. And Shane knew it. Shane didn't want her anymore, but he didn't want anyone else to have her either."

"What did you, Swolle, and Megan do while they raced?"

"Swolle didn't move off the dock. I didn't get far from it. I guess I joined him on it at one point so I could see them better. Megan raced with them—on her Jet Ski I mean. She was being so fuckin' nuts. She was all over the place. Almost hit them several times. I think she may have one time."

"I take medication for depression and ADD," Megan says. "I was upset and I was drinking. I got a little . . . I don't know . . . whacky."

"Why were you upset?" I ask.

"I don't know . . . It's just been a shitty few weeks. Life's so stinkin' hard sometimes. People are stupid. I've been feeling like Shane and I have been drifting apart. Then he comes into town and . . . not only am I not the first person he sees, he doesn't come see me at all. So I started drinkin' a little."

I nod.

"You're easy to talk to. Am I diggin' a hole for myself here? Underage drinkin' and all."

"Not at all. Is that all you were upset about?"

"No. Why?"

"What else?"

"Really? Well, my bitch of a greedy ex-grandmother canceled my Florida pre-paid college program she had been paying into and took the money out, so there's that."

"Ex-grandmother?"

"My dad's a creep. After he and my mom split, he and his psycho mother became dead to me."

"Why did she cancel your pre-paid tuition program?" I ask.

"Because I won't sit on her lap or kiss her ass or have anything to do with her. Because she's a greedy old bag. Take your pick. I don't know."

"Did you go to the Tupelo Festival?" I ask.

She nods.

"I thought I saw you. Did you see Shane and follow him to the landing?"

"I saw him. I didn't follow him. I knew where they were going . . . so I decided to bump into him, you know? Kinda cool like. I put my Jet Ski in at Iola and rode down to where they were. I say mine—it's mine now. My mom's ex-boyfriend left it behind when he moved on. Said he was coming back for it, but still hasn't."

"How'd Shane respond?"

"Shane's always nice. I could tell he wasn't thrilled I crashed his little boys' swimming party, but . . . he was pretty cool about it."

She starts to cry again.

"He was such a good guy. I can't believe he's gone."

"Tell me what happened? When and where was the last time you saw him?"

"It was just like they told you. They decided to leave. Matt was already out. Cody got out and started walking up the dock. Shane was still in the water. He and Cody had just had a race. He was winded. I was just sort of floating on the Jet Ski near him. I said, 'Well, guess I'll go now. You be sure to let me know if you ever want to see me, okay?' He said, 'Wait. Don't go. I need to talk to you.' He told me to pull around to the boat launch and tie up my Jet Ski. He'd give me a ride to my truck in Iola and we could talk. When I came up . . ."

She begins to cry again. Harder this time.

I hand her some tissues and wait.

"When I came up to the dock after I tied up my Jet Ski, Matt and Cody were looking for him. Asked if he was with me or if I knew where he was. I knew right then something was wrong. We started yelling for him. Looking. I called nine-one-one."

"Why didn't y'all get back into the water and look for him?"

"I did. I tried so hard to find him, but . . . it was so . . . I couldn't see anything. I kept feeling around but . . . I just couldn't . . ."

"Just you?"

She nods. "When I called nine-one-one, the guys panicked. They were too busy hiding their shit from the cops to help. We might have been able to save him if they hadn't been. Fuckin' selfish assholes."

"How did he seem the last time you saw him?" I ask. "Do you think maybe the swim had—"

"That damn race. So important to win. Do you think that could've been what . . . He didn't seem to feel too good. Looked pale and . . . He was breathing sort of heavy and said his head hurt, but he seemed okay. I wouldn't've left him if I thought he was anything but a little tired. But you should ask Cody. He's the one who was in the water with him."

Chapter Fourteen

"**I** think it may be my fault he's dead," Cody says. "We should've never raced like that. He took it so seriously. He pushed himself so hard. I could've beaten him, but I backed off and let him win. Even then he didn't slow down, didn't stop trying to prove he's some dumb fuckin' Marine. We just should've never done it."

"Whose idea was it?" I ask. "The race."

He shrugs and seems to think about it.

Cody has the build of a high school baseball player. Tall. Trim. Muscular, but in the longish way that lacks much in the way of definition. His green eyes beneath his short and wavy dirty blond hair are dull. He's cocky and entitled but like so many mama's boys around here, he has a finely honed faux humility, insincere deference to authority, and a manipulative Southern charm he can turn on at will.

"Sort of just happened," he says. "I'm not sure exactly. His, maybe, but it could've been Megan's. God, I just feel so dang bad about it. I know how he is. I shouldn't have agreed to race him. He'd probably still be alive."

I don't say anything, just listen.

He shakes his head. "I still can't believe he's gone. One second he's there in the water with us, the next he's . . .

he's just . . ."

"Gone?" I offer.

"Yeah."

Everything Cody says comes off as manipulative and insincere.

"Whatta you think happened to him?" I ask.

He seems to really consider my question.

"Most likely he caught a cramp and went under, got caught on something or a gator got him or he just couldn't get back to the surface and he drowned. Or . . . I think he hit his head—or got it hit. Maybe he was . . . you know . . . dazed . . . had a concussion or something like that."

"How'd he hit his head? What happened?"

"Just an accident."

"What was?"

"Megan was sort of racing with us, making big circles around us. She didn't mean to . . . it was just an accident, but . . . she got too close one time and hit Shane in the head. She felt horrible. It was a total fuckin' accident. Just one of those things, know what I mean?"

"He got hit in the head and still won the race?" I ask.

He lets out a harsh little laugh. "I guess he did. But like I said it was just a little hit and I backed off to let him win. It was just that he didn't slow down then. He kept going full force. He overdid it."

I nod.

"What happened to him could have nothing to do with the race," Cody says. "He could've just drowned. Gator could'a just come up and got 'im. Could'a just been his time, God's mysterious plan and all. I don't know. You just asked me what I thought *could* have happened."

"And I appreciate it. So why didn't you get back in

the water to look for him after y'all noticed he was missing?"

"Well . . . I . . . I wish I had. By God I really do. But at the time . . . I thought he was with Megan at first . . . then . . . I . . . I guess I just thought he'd pop up any minute, you know? Then Megan called you guys . . . and then I thought, well . . . and then she jumped in and started looking . . . and I . . . I don't know. I . . ."

"Had to hide your drugs and alcohol and—"

He frowns and begins to shake his head, his eyes moistening just a bit. "No. There's no way you found any of that shit in my truck. I'm clean. What? Did you plant some shit in my truck?"

"No, we found it in the bathroom where you hid it so you could come back for it later," I say.

"You find shit in the bathroom and you just assume it's mine, huh?"

"Not assumption," I say. "Fingerprints."

"Oh."

"What if I told you you had immunity for the drugs, that all I'm interested in is finding out what happened to Shane? Would you answer my question? Why didn't you go back into the water?"

"I . . . I panicked, all right? If I had known he was going to . . . I still thought he was going to be okay. I was doing it as much for him as the rest of us—more so. He could get kicked out of the army for . . . I was just trying to take care of everything for us. I'm working hard to get a baseball scholarship next year. I ain't tryin' to fuck that up."

"Not what it looks like to me."

"It was stupid, okay. I shouldn't've been doin' it, but I damn sure didn't want to get caught with it. I knew it could fuck up both of our futures," he says.

"Whose?"

"Mine and Shane's. The rest of them don't have anything to fuck up. I wasn't just thinking about myself. I was thinking about him too."

There's a knock at the door and Reggie leans her head in. "Sorry to interrupt. Can I borrow you a minute?"

Chapter Fifteen

"**H**ow's it goin'?"

I tell her.

"That fits with what I have," she says.

"What's that?"

"We found blood on Megan's Jet Ski. On the front. Could've been where she hit him."

I nod and think about it.

Reggie continues. "Could be why she was so shaken up. Question is . . . was it really an accident or did she mean to do it?"

"It may've had nothing to do with what happened to him," I say. "He finished the race—even won it, and seemed fine for a while after that. It could've contributed. It could have nothing to do with it. We won't know until we find his body and figure out exactly what happened to him. We don't even know if it's his blood."

"True. We do know it's human blood and it matches Shane's blood type, so it's probably his, but we won't know for sure until we find him and run the DNA. Just wanted you to know while you were still talking to them."

"Thanks. I appreciate it."

"I'm headed back down to the landing," she says.

"Call me if anything . . ."

"I'll see you down there when I finish up here."

"Did your Jet Ski strike Shane on the head?" I ask.

Megan breaks down and begins to sob.

I wait.

"Is that what killed him?" she asks eventually.

"Tell me what happened."

"It was just a stupid accident," she says, sniffling. "I was being stupid. I . . . I just wanted to show him I could be fun and free-spirited like whoever he's interested in now. I was showing off—the way they were. But I was buzzin' and my perception was a little off and I got too close and . . . well . . . I just barely grazed him. He seemed fine. Please, please, please tell me that's not what . . . killed him."

"Why didn't you mention it before?" I say.

"I've been trying to block it out," she says. "Part of me was hoping it really didn't happen at all, that I just . . . I don't know . . . imagined it. And I honestly didn't think it had anything to do with . . . anything."

"When did it happen?"

"During the race. What do you mean?"

"When exactly?"

"I don't know."

"Where were they—on the way over to the house-boat, on the way back? Closer to one side of the river than the other?"

"Oh. Only a little over halfway over on the way to the houseboat," she says. "I was being so stupid. I chilled after that, though. Stayed close to them in case they needed help and to watch for boats coming, but no more stupid stunts, no more trying to get his attention."

"So after it happened, he still swam half the way over and all the way back?"

"Yeah. Like I said, it was just a graze. Barely touched him. I think."

"But you couldn't really tell from up on the Jet Ski, could you?"

She hesitates. "No, I guess not. I . . . just . . . It didn't seem bad at all and he didn't act like it was and said he was fine. I asked him a lot. I tried to get him to quit the silly race and get on the Jet Ski with me, but . . . he said he didn't even feel it."

"**O**h, he felt it," Cody says. "He was trying to act all Rambo and shit. She could'a hit him with a fuckin' Mack Truck and he'a acted like it didn't hurt."

"But he was able to finish the race," I say. "And win."

"On pride, ego, and adrenaline, but yeah, he was. And maybe it really didn't hurt him. He acted fine. He just . . . always acted like nothing hurt him, so . . . you know . . . it was hard to tell."

"How long after the race was it before you got out of the river?"

"We stayed in for a while, sort of holding on to the dock and catching our breath, letting Shane brag about what a badass he is for . . . a few minutes. Ten maybe. I got out. Shane stayed in. It was the last time I ever saw him."

"How long between you getting out and y'all noticing he was missing?"

"I walked up the metal part of the dock, stopped on

the wooden platform, called a girl about a party that was supposed to take place last night out on Road 5. Talked to her a few minutes. Then walked the rest of the way up. I was tired. Moving slow. I don't know. Ten, fifteen minutes, maybe."

"How were you feeling?" I ask. "Besides tired. How were your muscles? Your head?"

"I was exhausted. Cramping. Hurting. Felt like shit."

"How much had y'all had to drink?" I say. "What all had y'all taken?"

"More than we should if we were going to do that stupid shit," he says. "I don't know. Maybe four or five beers."

"Each?"

"Each."

"Shane too?"

He nods.

"What else?"

"Some Xanbars."

A benzodiazepine used for the treatment of anxiety and insomnia, a Xanbar is a long thin pill that has four sections—essentially four Xanax per pill or bar. Taken with alcohol, it really relaxes the muscles, provides a nice tipsy buzz, and a very clean drunk.

"How much? The entire bar? A fourth of it? What?"

"We had a few. I don't know exactly how they got split up."

"Did Megan and Swolle have any?"

"Yeah."

"You sure?"

"Yeah. Why?"

"Because," I say, "memory loss is one of the main

side effects of it. Most people don't remember much of anything after taking it. Calls into question everything each of you has said."

"Well, I remember everything. I—"

"Did Shane take some of the Xanbar too?"

He nods. "He had at least one."

"One fourth or one whole bar?"

"One bar, I think."

"So with very relaxed muscles and a full-on drunk going, y'all swam across the river and back?"

"We felt good. It wasn't a—"

"And the drugs were yours?"

"You said it wasn't an issue," he says. "Said I had impunity."

"Immunity."

"Yeah."

"For the drug possession charge, sure," I say. "But not for Shane's death."

"Shane's death?"

"Sure. That much alcohol and drugs in his system. Probably what made him go under in the first place. Probably what caused him to drown."

My phone rings as he starts to object.

It's Reggie.

I step out of the conference room to take it.

"Can you pause the interviews and come to the landing?" she says. "Fast as you can."

"On my way. What's up?"

"We've got a body," she says. "But it's the wrong one. And it's bad."

Chapter Sixteen

Racing toward the river, I call Anna and tell her what's happening.

"So they found a body, but not Shane's?" she says.

"What it sounds like. She didn't say much."

"Wonder who it could be?" she says. "There haven't been any missing persons reports filed recently, have there?"

"There haven't."

"Who goes missing without anyone noticing? Or caring."

"Well find out."

"How'd the interviews go?"

I tell her.

"So stupid," she says.

"Which part?"

"All of it."

"Wonder how much of it even happened," I say. "If they took what Cody said they did, as much as he said they did, they wouldn't remember much."

We are quiet a moment.

Long before we were together I had discussed details of my cases with Anna, had always benefited from bouncing ideas around, having her listen and question and provide perspectives and insight, but now that we're together it's been taken to a whole new level. Now we share everything. Now she's who I call every free moment I have, in between everything, and she's who I get to go home to, climb into bed with, the one I get to whisper late into the night with.

"I'm so grateful to have you," I say. "To share everything with. And I will never take it for granted."

"Go ahead," she says, "take it for granted. I'm not going anywhere."

I smile. "Me either. Not willingly."

"Don't go anywhere," she says, "willingly or otherwise. Be careful. All the time."

"I am," I say. "Maybe even too careful these days."

"Good. Keep it that way. Are you at the landing yet or do you have a minute for me to tell you what I found? Actually it won't take but a second. Whatever Megan posted on Facebook or any other social media I could find is gone. Every bit of it erased. And it looks like the boys haven't posted anything. If they did, it's gone too. But what *is* on all of their pages and on their friends' pages are tons of comments and questions and even accusations about what happened. People are ripping Megan apart, calling her a stalker and a killer. The Jet Ski Assassin. The Apalachicola River Ripper."

"*Shit.* The stupid . . . ignorant . . . hateful . . . Social media is the new mob, isn't it?"

"All they need are emoticon pitchforks."

I arrive at the landing to find Reggie, Ralph, and a FWC officer named Nichols waiting for me.

They are standing near the mobile command unit.

"This is Nick Nichols with FWC," Reggie says. "This is John Jordan, my new investigator."

FWC is the Florida Fish and Wildlife Conservation Commission, the state agency in charge of managing and regulating Florida's wildlife and enforcing the pertinent laws. If there's a body in the river, they have jurisdiction.

"John," he says, extending his hand. "Nice to meet you."

"FWC has turned it over to us," Reggie says. "I've called in FDLE and the ME."

FDLE is the Florida Department of Law Enforcement, the state agency formed in 1967 that answers directly to the governor and is composed of five areas: Executive Direction and Business Support, Criminal Investigations and Forensic Science, Criminal Justice Information, Criminal Justice Professionalism, and Florida Capitol Police. FDLE works closely with local law enforcement, offering support and resources local agencies don't have.

The ME or medical examiner of the 14th Judicial District has offices in Panama City but covers Bay, Calhoun, Gulf, Holmes, Jackson, and Washington counties. His job is to provide medical examiner services, including investigations, autopsies, and the issuing of death certificates, to criminal justice, law enforcement, insurance agencies, funeral homes, and the general public.

"Turned over what?" I say. "What do we have?"

Ralph says, "Our side-scan sonar found a body on

the bottom. Cadaver dog confirmed. We dragged the area. Hooked the body. Thought it was the McMillan boy at first, but it's not. When we got it to the surface and saw what we had, we left it right there and called y'all. Usually we gather the boats around so the family or media can't see anything, then load the body—we have a boat with a side gate we can pull the body right up onto—then we take it to the next landing down so the family doesn't see it in that condition. But when it's an obvious homicide, we stop right where we are—because at that point the body is the crime scene— and we don't do anything else until y'all tell us to."

My question still hasn't been answered.

"So we have an obvious homicide victim that's not Shane?" I say.

"We have a ritualistic sexual killing," Reggie says. "Female victim. Been in the water a while. Maybe a week. Maybe more."

"Never seen anything like it," Ralph says. "And I've been doin' this a while."

"None of us have," Reggie says.

Nick shakes his head. "That poor girl."

"Her poor parents," Reggie adds.

"What did he do to her?"

Ralph rushes to get it out and I can't tell if it's because of what he's saying or because he wants to be the one to say it. "Fashioned a metal bar cross and crucified her face down on it and made it so that it's fuckin' her."

Chapter Seventeen

While we're waiting for FDLE and the ME to arrive, I start to walk across the landing to where Tommy is standing, but I stop when I see the sad look on Ralph's face, the vacant stare in his eyes.

"You okay?"

He nods, pursing his lips and narrowing his eyes.

"Just . . . I . . . Every time we find something down here . . . *every single time* . . . I expect it to be Ronnie. I know it's crazy. Wouldn't be anything but bones now, but . . . I just keep hoping. Just keep looking."

I put my hand on his shoulder. "I'm so sorry. I can't even begin to imagine what you go through every time you're out here helping others."

He squeezes his eyes shut tight, a little moisture popping out on each side, and swallows hard.

"Thank you," he says. "I'm okay. I'll be okay. I just . . . I don't want people to forget him. I don't even care if they call him Red Face Raffield. Just don't forget him, don't forget he's down there somewhere."

Tommy is near the picnic pavilion rehydrating before returning to searching for Shane.

When he sees me, he starts in my direction, putting us well away from anyone else.

We hug and I ask how he's doing.

"Numb," he says. "Just past the point, you know? Sure it's a combination of shock, grief, and exhaustion."

I nod and frown and express my sympathy again.

He looks around us, then lowers his voice a little. "I heard they found something. Is it Shane?"

I follow his gaze out to the spot where the three search and rescue boats are gathered waiting for us.

When he looks back at me I shake my head.

"They didn't find something or it's not Shane?"

"It's not Shane."

Tears fill his eyes again. "They won't tell me much. And the only help they let me provide is way away from the main search."

They don't want you finding him, I think. I don't want you to either.

"They got me searching the woods, following the sandy hills down to the banks."

I nod. "I'll tell you anything I can," I say. "Anything I find out. But just know if you're not told something, no one is keeping information about Shane from you. There just isn't any yet."

"Speaking of information," he says. "Have you heard what people are sayin' in town and on Facebook?"

"What?"

"All kinds of stuff. That Megan killed him, actually ran over him with her Jet Ski. That all of them did it or maybe it was an accident, but they are covering it up together. That Shane was part of some secret military project and was assassinated and that's why there's no body."

"I'm so sorry you have to hear all that," I say. "I promise when there's something real I'll tell you."

"Thanks."

When I get back to the group, the FDLE agent has arrived.

The FDLE agent's name is Samantha Michaels. She goes by Sam. She's slight—blonde, pale, petite, diminutive—but carries herself as if she's not.

"I know you," she says, her blue eyes wide, her head cocked to the side when we're introduced. "Used to be the chaplain at PCI."

"Yeah?" I say, curious.

In the distance, near the kids' playground, the FDLE crime scene unit pulls up and techs jump out and begin to set up.

"Should've said I know *of* you," Sam says. "Was told you recaptured the Phoenix when he escaped. I interviewed him for a case I was working on in the Bayshore Pine Key area. Had a ritualistic killer using fire as a weapon. Went to talk to the Phoenix about it. Fucker set me on fire in the interview room at the prison."

"I remember," I say.

"How the hell'd he do that?" Reggie asks.

"With a single match and a tube of accelerant," she says. "Mostly just burned my hair off, but it was traumatic."

"You caught the guy who was making burnt offerings of his victims," I say. "That was very impressive."

Though muscular and hard-bodied, she is so small,

so pale, it's hard to imagine her fighting, let alone slaying dragons.

"Just gave him a little taste of his own weapon," she says.

"You burned him?" Reggie says, her eyes widening as her brows shoot up.

Ralph smiles and says, "That mean you'll crucify this sick fuck?"

Chapter Eighteen

We are joined by the ME, a big-bellied balding black man, and a thin young white FDLE tech, and the seven of us walk down the dock and board the boat very near where Shane was when he vanished.

Of the seven of us, Samantha Michaels looks out of place. So small she looks more like an as-yet-to-develop early adolescent girl than an actual adult—an adult with authority and expertise and a gun and a badge.

Often the medical examiner's office sends an investigator to the scene, but for this, the ME himself has come. Though FWC has jurisdiction over the water and turned it over to the sheriff's department, and she has called in FDLE, the ME has jurisdiction over the body. And once he has finished his initial examination at the scene, it will be him who tags the body and follows the funeral home that will be transporting it back to his office or the morgue, and it will be him who conducts the autopsy.

Once we are in and seated or holding on, the search and rescue driver ferries us the short distance out to where the three other boats are creating a barrier around the body.

Pulling up in the rear to form the fourth wall that

frames the body, the driver tosses the anchor over and ties up to the two boats nearest us.

And then we behold the horror.

The side gate on our boat is opened, lowering into the water, and the decaying body and the sacrilegious cross it's attached to are hoisted on board.

"Oh my God," Reggie says.

Both metal beams of the cross are small, narrow, and rectangular.

The body is bolted to it face down, wrists at the ends of the crossbar, ankles together at the bottom of the upright bar. At various other places, including the neck, twisted strands of barbed wire eat into the pale naked flesh as they help secure body to beams.

Young. Naked. Thin. Streaks of river bottom mud smear her skin and matt her hair.

Someone's little girl. Someone's kid sister. Someone's best friend. Someone's girlfriend.

Something precious to someone. Living. Breathing. Dreaming. Laughing. Planning.

Now decaying. Now desecrated. Now defiled. Now dead. Now discarded.

Purplish patches of fixed lividity on her back, butt, and calves. Various abrasions—many most likely from her time at the bottom of the river.

Post mortem lividity occurs when a person's heart stops beating and blood pools in the lowest parts of the body, causing purplish bruising patters on the skin. After eight to twelve hours the lividity becomes fixed and doesn't change even if the body is moved.

The FDLE tech takes pictures and the ME does a quick examination of the body, then he and Ralph and

I disconnect the search and rescue drag hooks, most of which, thankfully, are attached to the crossbars, and carefully turn her over.

The front is far worse and far more difficult to look at.

Seeing the young girl, I can't help but imagine Johanna or Taylor in her place.

Reggie grabs my upper arm and squeezes as she looks down, and I reach up and over and cover her hand with mine.

Her head is held so tightly to the beam by the barbed wire around her neck and forehead that the bar had made an indentation in her face and forehead.

Lifeless blue eyes, wide open and wet, stare out of either side of the metal beam, looking up, seeing nothing.

A thick ring of barbed wire strands form a crown of thorns on her head.

Small breasts, barely rising in her prone position, their nipples pale and pink nearly nonexistent, make her look all the more vulnerable, all the more exposed, all the more in need of care and cover.

An anklet tattoo of vines and flowers and birds around her left ankle.

Both fingernails and toenails painted. Though different colors.

Ligature marks around her neck.

A large, wet wound in her side is meant to approximate the spear that pierced Jesus.

But of all the shocking and horrific aspects of this complete and utter violation, the most unsettling is the metal bar extending up at a forty-five-degree angle and disappearing into her fully exposed, clean-shaven vagina.

The ME takes more pictures and does a cursory examination.

We all stand as silent witnesses to the unfathomable and unspeakable act, no one moving, no one looking away.

Like the back, the bars are solid—except for a few holes about an inch in diameter on the right end of the crossbar.

When the ME is finished, Sam Michaels squats down next to the victim and touches her cheek with the tips of her gloved fingers.

"You just rest now, sweetheart," she says. "We're going to get the monster who did this evil thing to you. We're gonna make sure he never does this to any other innocent girl like yourself again. I promise you that."

Behind her we are all nodding—even the ME, FDLE tech, and the search and rescue driver.

Chapter Nineteen

"It doesn't even seem real," Reggie is saying. "I mean . . . *fuck*."

She, Sam, and I are back at the landing, standing well away from everyone else.

"We went from wondering if our accidental drowning was truly accidental to . . . this . . . to the sickest, most sadistic shit I've ever even heard about."

Sam says, "Y'all both know that was way too specific and sophisticated to be his first time."

I nod.

"A goddamn serial killer," Reggie says. "In my backyard."

In one sense she means figuratively—this is all of our backyard—but in another she's being very literal. She lives in a trailer with her mom on Byrd Parker Drive—just the third place down from the landing, her backyard, which I can see from here, backs up to the river, less than a hundred yards from where the body was discovered.

"There's no telling how far the body traveled," I say. "It could've been dumped upstream and drifted down here."

Given the weight of the cross, I know it's doubtful,

but in theory it's possible.

"But," I continue, "even if he dumped the body here, it doesn't mean he's local."

"This could be his dumping ground," Sam says. "We'll see if any other bodies show up. Or she could be from here. He just passes through, works his way up and down the river. It may be full of bodies. Any missing persons matching . . . any teenage girls missing?"

Reggie shakes her head. "Not from here—not from either end of the county."

"Identifying her will really help," Sam says. "Hope we'll be able to. Then we need to see if we can find similar cases, see if there are any suspects already."

I nod. "And not just in Florida."

"There's a religious element," she adds. "I know you have a religious background, John, but I'd like to bring in my husband to consult too. He's a former religion professor—now a profiler who specializes in this sort of thing."

"I attended a workshop he did at UF in Gainesville," I say. "He'd be a real asset for us."

"I want you two working on this together, with my help," Reggie says. "Can you do that, John, and continue the investigation into Shane's death?"

I nod.

As the chief law enforcement officer in the county, it's Reggie's call. FDLE is here at her invitation. By pairing us, we'll have the resources of FDLE and our knowledge of all things local. Having FDLE involved will also help with any jurisdictional issues if the investigation takes us out of Gulf County.

"We're not thinking they're related, right?" Reggie says.

I shake my head. "Don't see how they could be so far, but . . . we'll keep an eye out for any connections."

Sam nods, then turns to Reggie. "Were you saying you didn't want Daniel consulting?"

"What? When?"

"When I mentioned him you said you wanted me and John to work on it with you."

"Oh. No. Sorry. We'll use all the support staff we can—from forensics to deputies—I was just making sure it wasn't too much for John and that our departments can work together on it."

Reggie seems off and I wonder if she's shaken up from seeing the victim or feeling the weight of the responsibility of such a case or if it's something else.

"Good. I was asking because it's not official. He just helps me, but I want to be able to bring him along if I need to—to a crime scene or meeting or whatever."

"Sure. Great. Yeah."

"Hopefully we'll get a match on other cases," Sam says. "Hard to imagine forensics is going to be able to give us much."

"Given what we have now," I say to Reggie, "can you get search and rescue to widen their search?"

She nods. "Absolutely."

"And I know this is shocking and horrific and extraordinary," I say, "but I don't want it to overshadow our investigation into what happened to Shane."

Reggie nods enthusiastically. "Make sure it doesn't," she says. "You're in charge of making sure it doesn't."

While Reggie talks to Ralph about expanding the search, Sam and I figure out our next move.

"Is she okay?" Sam asks.

"I don't know what's going on," I say. "She was definitely a little off. She's normally more together than that. She's a good sheriff. I'm sure she'll be fine tomorrow."

She nods. "I look forward to working with you on this," she says.

"Same here. I really appreciate what you said to the victim."

"I meant it."

"I know you did. And you were speaking for all of us."

"So . . ." she says, "what's your initial take on the crucifixion element?"

"He made it part of his sexual sadism," I say, "but the cross is a symbol of both sacrifice and suffering—and ultimately to a symbol of redemption for some. He's making her suffer, of course, but for what? He's making a sacrifice of her, but for what? His sin? Hers? Is she a sacrifice because she's pure, or because she's wicked and deserves to die? In a way, what he's done is crucifying and then baptizing. Is that intentional, symbolic in some way for him, or just a way to hide the body and help wash away evidence? Why a metal cross instead of wood? Why bolts instead of nails? And his use of barbed wire . . . are all these things convenient or significant? My guess is significant, and figuring out how will help us find him."

"Like I said," she says with a smile, "I'm *really* looking forward to working with you on this."

"Just a lot of questions."

"They're the right questions," she says. "Which is

the key in any investigation. Probably be redundant to ask Daniel to consult, but—"

"Not at all," I say. "He knows so much more about all this than me. I'd love the chance to get to work with him. And I think we'll need all the help we can get on this one."

She nods slowly, thoughtfully. "I'm afraid you're right."

We are quiet a moment.

Eventually she says, "I really don't see how your missing swimmer and our victim can be connected. Am I missing something?"

I shrug. "I tend to agree. Be hard to see how they could be, but . . . can't rule it out entirely yet either. Same landing. So close together. Maybe Shane saw something. Maybe the killer took him out because of it."

"Maybe," she says. "Maybe *he's* the killer. Maybe that's why he was swimming here—to be close to her."

"Even less likely, but maybe."

"Okay," she says. "There's not much for us to do yet. Why don't you continue working on your swimmer case and I'll check ViCAP for matching victims and missing persons. We'll see what the prelim tells us in the morning and go from there."

ViCAP or the Violent Criminals Apprehension Program is the FBI's unit responsible for the analysis of serial violent and sexual crimes—a system Sam has access to through FDLE.

"If you find anything, don't wait until tomorrow," I say. "Call me tonight."

Chapter Twenty

Still shaken, Reggie calls Merrick.

"Where are you?" she asks.

"Home."

"Mine or yours?"

They live less than a mile apart and use both equally and refer to both as home.

"Mine. You okay? What's wrong? Did you find Shane?"

"I need to talk to you," she says. "And I need to trust you more than I ever have anyone."

"You can."

"Meet me in my backyard?" she says.

"On my way."

"Have you seen Rain?" she asks.

"Not since this morning when you did. Why?"

"I can't get him to answer his phone."

They are sitting in the swing in her backyard, overlooking the Apalachicola River. The wooden swing hangs between posts that give a little in the loose dirt around them as it moves. Out in the water, search and rescue boats move about searching for Shane. One with a cadaver dog on the bow, one with the side-scan sonar taking images every fifteen feet or so. Two dragging the bottom. And an unseen observation pontoon boat now five miles down.

"What's going on?" he says. "Tell me so I can help."

"I've already trusted you far more than anyone else ever," she says.

"Don't stop now."

She takes a deep breath, holds it a moment, then lets it out slowly. "We found a girl in the river," she says, and proceeds to tell him what happened.

"My God," he says. "That's . . . fuck. That's . . ."

She realizes that she had been in this same damn swing when she had the most difficult conversation of her adult life. It was this swing she fell into after the devastating dawning of revelation in her last case.

She should burn this fuckin' swing. Of course it's not like bad news and difficult conversations and painful realizations would cease if this swing ceased to exist. And besides . . . there is something comforting about it, something solid—as if it has the strength and density to absorb pain and sadness, guilt and shame.

"No wonder you're so upset," he says.

"It was bad, but that's not why I'm . . . so . . . I . . . Here's where the trust comes in."

"Okay."

"I think it's Amber," she says.

"Amber?"

"Matthews," she adds.

"The little girl Rain was seeing?" he asks, his voice rising.

She looks around.

"Sorry," he says, lowering his voice again. "The one who ghosted him?"

"The one we thought ghosted him."

"How long has she been . . ."

"About the time she disappeared on him."

"So the texts she sent him . . ."

"Probably sent by her killer."

"Her boyfriend who answered her phone?"

"The killer."

"He's going to be devastated," he says.

"Devastated, I can deal with. Implicated, not so much."

"How?"

"First I want to confirm it's her. I need to see the pictures he has of her again. Then I need to know the details of their relationship and last day together, and then account for his whereabouts ever since."

You should hear what they're saying," Tommy says. "About the body y'all found. It's all anyone can talk about."

"It was bad."

We are standing on the end of the dock, looking out at the activity in the water. Reggie, Sam, and Ralph have all gone.

It's evening. Quieter and cooler now.

Behind us the landing is mostly empty. A few search and rescue support staff. A single deputy posted at the entrance.

"I feel real bad for that little girl," he says. "Already been praying for her and her family. And I hope y'all catch whoever did it quick so he can never do anything like it again."

I wait, knowing there is more.

"But . . . it's hard not to resent her some too. It's like everybody has forgotten about Shane. It's like him still being missing is a distant second because he's not the victim of some serial killer or something."

"I can see how it would feel that way," I say, "but it's not the case. Those boats out there right now, they're searching for Shane. I spent most of the afternoon interviewing his friends who were with him. The sheriff, FDLE, and I have already talked about not letting the discovery of the body today take anything away from our search for Shane and our investigation into exactly what happened to him."

He nods. "Thank you. I feel so . . . childish for feeling resentful of that poor girl, but . . . I just want my boy to be treated like he should, like he deserves."

"I promise you that will be the case," I say.

"Thank you. That's all I needed to hear."

Chapter Twenty-one

I arrive home to discover we have an unexpected but not unwelcome dinner companion.

Since losing his job, my dad had been just sort of drifting aimlessly, and my sweet Anna had invited him to dinner often, and though he often declined the invitation, when he did join us it seemed to do him good.

"I hope you don't mind," Anna whispers when I walk into the kitchen.

Dad is in the living room giving Taylor a bottle.

"Of course not. I appreciate you doing it."

"I know how much you're dealing with right now."

"I'm glad you invited him. Glad he actually came."

"I invited Merrill and Jake too, but they're both working."

Merrill Monroe is my best friend and Jake Jordan is my younger brother. I'd be surprised if Jake came, but I'm disappointed Merrill can't make it. I miss him. Since we moved and I took the new jobs, I have seen far less of him—and my life is the lesser for it.

We eat.

Anna has prepared parmesan chicken, potatoes, and

my favorite—fresh field peas and fried cornbread—and it is truly delicious, nourishing me in many ways.

After dinner and after Taylor is down, Dad, Anna, and I wind up in my library—Anna with wine, Dad with a beer, and me with sweet tea.

In my previous home—an old single wide house trailer in Pottersville—I had books in every room, in piles and stacks, on the floors against the walls. Here, in our new home, at Anna's insistence, I have a proper library in the converted formal living room, and I love it.

"Still no sign of the McMillan boy?" Dad says.

He's sitting on a small antique-looking love seat that had been his mother's.

I shake my head. Not yet.

Anna is in a chair across from him.

I'm on the rug on the floor between them, a book about religious symbolism and homicide in my lap. During breaks in our conversation, I glance down and quickly take in short passages.

The concept of sacrifice means to make holy and carries the connotation of a religious practice in its fullest, most complete sense. It can best be understood in the context of its four historical purposes: homage, thanksgiving, supplication, and expiation. Homage is an act of absolute adoration. Thanksgiving is appreciation for an answered prayer. Supplication is a request or petition for a gift, favor, or divine intervention. Expiation is a payment for sins committed, an attempt at placating divine anger and wrath. The desired result of such religious sacrifice is transformation, communion, regeneration, divine assimilation, and immortality.

"I hear what was found was really bad," Dad says.

"Maybe the worst I've ever seen," I say.

"Really?" Anna asks.

I nod.

"That's saying something," she says. "What exactly was it?"

I tell them.

"Oh my God," she says. "That poor child."

Dad shakes his head.

"I was thinking about it," I say. "Thinking about all the homicide victims I've seen over the years—the kids in Atlanta, the inmates in the prison, the women killed by the Stone Cold Killer at Stone Mountain, even the exorcism victims at the retreat center near Mexico Beach, which involved a crucifixion—and as truly tragic and terrible as all of them were, none of them were as elaborate and sadistic as what I witnessed today."

"I'm so sorry, baby," Anna says. "I wish you would've said something sooner."

"Nothing to say. Not really."

Dad says, "Worst ones I ever saw were victims of Bundy. Well, were said to be victims of Bundy's killing spree through the Panhandle. I have my doubts about one of them actually being his."

"Really?" I say. "A copycat? I didn't know you thought that about one of them."

"I'm actually taking another look at it now that I have all this free time. Why I told Reggie I wouldn't be able to accept her kind offer to consult for her department. I always said I'd reopen it one day. Just didn't realize it would take decades."

"That's great," Anna says. "Let us know if we can help in any way with it."

Research into the role of sacrifice in human history is extremely informative and relevant to contemporary ritual killings.

There is an undeniable link between accounts of historical ritual murder and blood rites and modern ritualistic crimes, which points to similar motivations, goals, and justifications.

Glasses empty, each exhausted from the day, we walk Dad to the door and say good-night.

As Anna and I prepare for bed, I walk through the house checking the doors and windows and turning off fans and lights.

In my library, I pause for a moment and read one final passage for the night.

Human sacrifice has been a widespread and complex practice throughout history—from blood rituals to cannibalism to ritual murder. The incontrovertible evidence is clear. The ideology behind the practice of sacrifice and sacrificial rituals is that blood is life and contains the life force and energy necessary for life, and shedding it, offering it, constitutes the highest offering possible. Both bloodletting and ingesting blood from a victim represents a reception of pure power, and the longer the victim is tortured, the longer the pain is prolonged, the more life, energy, and power is emitted. In this way, ritualistic torture and homicide become a modern act of human sacrifice, an act that is for the murderer/priest a sacred communion in which the power of life is assimilated and regenerated.

Later that night as I am making love to Anna, I see the crucified girl when I close my eyes.

"Look at me," I say.

She looks up at me and our eyes lock.

"You okay?"

"Just need to see into your soul right now."

"I swear it feels like you're making love to my soul when you look at me like that."

119

Chapter Twenty-two

On Monday morning, while Anna is filing papers to petition for paternity and a temporary restraining order against Susan in Leon County, I am with Sam Michaels and Reggie in Reggie's office behind the Gulf County Courthouse in Port St. Joe.

Located on the opposite end of the county from Wewa, Port St. Joe is a coastal town and the county seat.

"We've got a lot to cover," Reggie says, "so let's get started. I've got some things I need to share with you, but I'd like to do that last."

She looks like she hasn't slept. Her tired eyes are bloodshot and underscored by large, dark, purple half-moons, her face pale and puffy.

"Let's start with Shane. I've spoken with a Sergeant Foster from Fort Benning. Since this happened here while Shane was on leave, the army won't really be involved in the investigation. They do want updates—notifications of our findings, that sort of thing, but that's about it. The search continues. Nothing yet. Ralph says sometimes the bodies move and it makes it difficult to find them, but not to worry, they will. This is just the third day and they've gone as many as thirty-two before."

A tap at the door brings three coffees and the shy smile of the non-sworn young civilian receptionist.

The sheriff's department is behind the courthouse—between it and the jail—and Reggie's office is in the back of it.

Still fairly spartan, as if emphasizing how temporary it will be, the walls are mostly bare, her desk mostly empty. Pictures of her mom, Rain, and Merrick and her name plate on the desk are the only clues to whose office it actually is.

"I know we're not thinking there's a connection between Shane and . . . the crucifixion victim, but . . . there might wind up being one, so I'd like to go over what we have with you here," Reggie says to Sam.

Sam nods, her shoulder-length blond hair swinging a bit as she does. "I'd prefer that. You never know what might be *the* thing one of us needs to hear to connect to some other thing we know."

She's so small I wonder if her feet would touch the floor if she leaned all the way back in her chair.

"John?" Reggie says.

I tell them about the interviews and what came out of them. Looking back and forth at them the way I am highlights the stark contrast between them—Reggie so dark, Sam so pale, Reggie so much larger than Sam, Reggie's stern face, Sam's default pleasant expression.

"So," Reggie says, "we've got the contributing factors of the bump on the head from the Jet Ski, the drugs and alcohol, and the foolish swim across the river and back."

"Except that the Xanbar they took should mean they can't remember anything much about it," I say.

121

"Think they're all lying?" Sam asks, her blue eyes wide beneath raised brows.

"I don't know. I want to interview them again at some point. I was just hoping to have the body and the evidence it provides before I do."

"But," Reggie says, "even with the bump to the head, the exhaustion from the swim, and the effects of the substances, we're still most likely looking at an accidental drowning."

"Maybe," I say. "We need to find the body."

She nods then turns to Sam. "How about the results of the prelim autopsy on the body we did find?"

"As you can imagine, the water washed away any evidence we had hoped to find, and the state of decay makes it far more difficult to determine much, but—" she flips through a few pages in her narrow note pad "—all of the crucifixion stuff was done postmortem."

"That's something to be grateful for," Reggie says. "Not much, but something."

"She appears to have been sexually assaulted and to have died of ligature strangulation. Don't have much more than that at this point. We'll have more after the full autopsy, toxicology, and DNA testing, but I was told it most likely won't be much more. No ID yet. And my ViCAP searches haven't turned up any matches on missing persons or similar crimes, but I just know in my marrow this is not his first time."

"Think we all agree on that," Reggie says.

"I'm gonna keep searchin'," she says. "Widen my search. I'm gonna find his previous victims."

"Unless they're still at the bottom of the river," I say.

"What about the way she was staged?" Reggie says.

"It's a hell of a signature," Sam says.

"And will probably make it easier for us to catch him," I say. I then tell them more about the meaning and import of sacrifice in religious ritual killings.

"Daniel was saying some of those same things last night," Sam says. "We're dealing with one sick twisted fuck. Look forward to taking him off the board."

Reggie nods. "Okay, now to the hard part. This isn't easy for me, puts me in a very difficult spot, but I know we can find our way through it."

She pauses and we wait, a moment fraught with tension and piqued interest passing between us.

"I'm pretty sure I've figured out the identity of our victim. Her name is Amber Matthews. She's seventeen and she went missing a little over a week ago."

She hands us each a file folder with Amber Matthews's information and pictures in it.

"The pictures are printouts from Facebook and a few of her friends' phones," she says. "See the anklet tattoo? And I think this one is the last one ever taken of her. I'm pretty sure that's what she was wearing when she was taken."

Amber Matthews is a pretty girl, and it's truly difficult to conceive that the poor creature we pulled from the river once looked like this.

She poses for the camera the way so many young girls do these days, like models in training, showing off her outfit and accessories, smiling in a way that looks more unsure and insecure than happy.

She and Rain lying on a sheet in the sand at the beach. Her standing in front of a bonfire, a beer in one hand, giving the bird with the other. She and Rain sharing cotton candy at the carnival. A shot of her from the side taking a chocolate-covered banana into her mouth like she's going down on it.

Unlike her mouth and the rest of her face, her eyes aren't smiling. They are sad and wounded and wary—just not wary enough to keep her from getting too close to whoever snatched, killed, and crucified her.

Dressed to go out, she is wearing a sandstone cami tank top, blue jeans shorts with lace around the legs, sandals, and a headband that matches her top. Her long legs are smooth and shapely and show the first faint hints of a tan. Her long, narrow feet are in brown sandals and her anklet tattoo is clearly visible.

Hanging from a cord around her neck, a teardrop-shaped rose quartz hangs just above where her sandstone cami starts.

"Her phone has been used since she died so I've already sent a preservation letter to Verizon—her cell provider—and I've also been working with them to ping it to find the location, but it's been off. If it's turned back on and we can get a location, I'll let you know."

"This is great," Sam says. "But how'd you make the ID? How did you even first figure out it was her?"

"Because," Reggie says, "she was dating Rain, my son."

Chapter Twenty-three

Rain is saying, "I'm sad and upset, you know what I'm sayin', but I'm also . . . I don't know . . . a little . . . I'm . . . I'm glad I wasn't ghosted."

Getting ghosted by an ex is when they vanish out of your life and block you on all social media with no explanation. They just disappear and ignore all your efforts to contact them because you are dead to them and they are dead to you.

"She didn't seem like the type to do somethin' like that," Rain continues, "but . . . I didn't know her long or very well, so . . ."

We are in the sheriff's department's small interview room —Sam and me on one side of the desk, Rain and Merrick McKnight on the other.

The investigations office is behind the supervisor of elections office on Long Avenue—a mile or so from the sheriff's department, courthouse, and jail. The interview room is equipped with a hidden camera inside what appears to be a smoke detector.

I remember something from the Tupelo Festival.

"She didn't ghost you," I say. "She was murdered. So . . . if the person who answered her phone on Saturday wasn't her boyfriend . . . it could be the killer."

His eyes grow wide as the blood drains from his face. His eyes aren't as striking as his mom's and they're more squinty, but it's obvious he's her son.

"What did he sound like?" I say.

He shrugs. "I don't know. Quiet. Sort of soft spoken."

"Young? Older? Southern?"

"Yeah," he says, nodding. "Young and from the South."

"How long did you date?" Sam asks.

"Let's see . . . she moved here during Christmas break. I had a girlfriend at the time. We broke up not too long before Valentine's Day, 'cause I was like, why not before I spent all that money on candy and gifts, you know what I'm saying? Then I kicked it solo for a month or more. Amber and me started talkin' on April first. I remember 'cause I made a joke about her not prankin' me 'cause it was April Fool's Day. She went away spring break. We became exclusive sometime end of April, beginning of May."

"What can you tell us about her?" I ask.

"Probably not much, you know what I'm sayin'? Didn't know her long. She was cool. No drama. We just hung out. Had fun. Between school, basketball, then baseball and helping take care of my grandma, I didn't have a ton of time. Her mom split when she was little. I know that. She lived with her dad and his new family in Dothan, but her stepmom was a real bitch and her stepbrother and sister real brats. So she left. Seemed like they didn't even care. She moved here to get away from them. Lived with an old lady who kept her mom when she was young. She was like an aunt but not really, know what I'm sayin'?"

126

We are quiet a moment and he tears up again. Wiping his eyes with his thumb and forefinger, he sniffles and pats his foot. Beside him, Merrick puts a hand on his shoulder.

"Rain, did your mom tell you not to tell us anything?" Sam asks.

He shakes his head. "She told me to tell y'all everything I know. I didn't . . . I haven't done anything wrong and she knows it. Got nothin' to hide. She said she doesn't know you all that well, but that John will do the right thing by me."

"He will," she says, nodding, "and so will I."

"So when's the last time you heard from Amber and when's the last time you saw her?" I ask.

"Saturday before the Tupelo Festival," he says. "We spent nearly the whole day together. Did all kinds of things. Ended up at a party at Iola Landing."

Merrick's eyes widen, mirroring mine.

"What?" Sam says. "What is it?"

"Iola is the landing just above Gaskin Park," I say.

If she was put in the water there, she could have drifted down along the bottom and gotten hung up on something where we found her.

"Tell me about the party," I say.

"Just the usual. Big fire. Everybody standing around talking and drinking."

"Did you drink?" Sam asks.

"Yes, ma'am. I know my mom will hear this. I'm sorry, Mom, but I did. But I only had two beers. I was going to have one, but we stayed a while so I had two."

"Take anything?" she asks.

"No ma'am. I never have and I never will."

"How about Amber?" I ask.

"Not that I know of—I mean, she had a beer or two. I didn't see her take anything."

"It's mostly young people your age at these parties, right?" I say.

"Yes, sir."

"What about that night? Anyone older there? Anyone you didn't recognize? Anyone acting creepy or—"

"No, sir. Was just us. The usual group. Wasn't many of us that night. Everybody there was our age. All people we knew. Wait. There was one kid from St. Joe. He's our age, but he's not one of us. He plays basketball for them."

"You ever see him at a party before?" I ask.

"No sir."

"What's his name?"

"Furnell Gant."

"Anything out of the ordinary happen that night? Anything unusual? Anything at all?"

"No sir. Just wasn't much to it. Tell the truth, it was kind of boring. I was tired from all we had done that day. So was Amber. She got real sleepy. She's the type that goes and goes but when she's done, she's done. Once she decides she's ready for bed, nothin's gonna stop her from going home and gettin' in bed."

"So y'all left?" I say. "Together?"

"No sir. She wanted me to take her home, but . . . I couldn't. I wanted to, but I just couldn't yet, so—"

"Why couldn't you?" Sam says.

"My mom's the sheriff," he says. "And she raised me right. By herself too, know what I'm sayin'? She's told me things. Taught me things. Made me the man I am, know what I'm sayin'? I'm not ever gonna let her down. Not

128

ever."

"What's that got to do with—"

"I've never had more than a beer or two. And I nurse the shit out of 'em. Lot of times I won't even finish them. Sometimes I pour them out when I go into the woods to pee. But even when I drink, I never have more than one in an hour and I always wait at least an hour since I've had one to drive. I told Amber to be patient. I just had to wait twenty-five more minutes, but . . . she wouldn't wait. Rode home with one of her friends. At first I thought that's why she wasn't responding to me the next day, thought she was mad about me not being able to take her home, but she's the one who said have another beer, let's stay a while longer, then just a little while later wanted to leave."

"What's her friend's name?" Sam asks. "The one who gave her the ride home?"

"Angel."

"Angel what?"

"Angel Keller. She's a senior."

Chapter Twenty-four

"When do you think Reggie knew who the victim was?" Sam asks.

We are in my car, driving down Highway 71 toward Wewa to interview Angel Keller at Wewa High School while Reggie tries to track Amber's phone and get in touch with her dad.

"On the boat yesterday," I say.

"And she waits until this morning to tell us. Why?"

"To look into it herself. To see what she needs to do to protect her son."

"You know if he had anything to do with it, we'll never be able to make a case. And if he didn't, any good defense attorney can cast suspicion on him and his mom's handling of the case and use him as an alternative suspect to get the real killer off."

I don't respond, just think about what she's saying.

"I know she's your boss, but . . . for fuck sake."

I nod. "I understand why she did what she did," I say, "but you're right. She just made our job a lot harder."

"We're screwed."

"Not necessarily," I say. "If the killer has done this before, which we all think he has, then we'll have several pattern cases and won't have to rely on Amber alone for the burden of proof."

"Let's hope so. 'Cause if not, we're screwed."

We are quiet for a few moments.

"How well do you know her?" Sam asks.

"Reggie? Haven't known her long. Just starting to get to know her. Why?"

"That dick move she did . . . makes me wonder," she says.

"What's that?"

"If the rumors around her last big case—the one that got her this job—are true."

"What have you heard?"

"Lots of unanswered questions," she says. "Suspicions of some sort of cover up. She had history with the victims. They started dying when she moved back to town. You should look into it?"

"Already am."

Walking down the covered walkway toward the double glass doors of WHS, me towering over her, Sam says, "Smell that? That smell like teen spirit to you?"

"Boredom and desperation," I say. "Monotony, banality, caste system, and conformity."

"That about covers it," she says. "Sounds like we had about the same high school experience."

Stepping aside and holding the door open for Sam, I can't help but think she looks more like a student entering the building than what she actually is.

Just before we walk in, she says, "Hey, you're a prison chaplain. What's worse, prison or high school?"

"High school. Not even close."

Entering the building, I'm reminded just how much like prison high school really is.

A smiling, upbeat, energetic, youngish teacher is waiting for us.

"Good morning," she says.

"Morning," I say.

"You're here to talk to Angel, right? Come this way. I've got a quiet corner in an empty classroom where you won't be disturbed."

"Thank you," I say.

The halls are empty, the kids all in classrooms. Everything is red and white—the school colors. Everywhere you look there is a gator—the school mascot.

"You seem really upbeat for a high school teacher," Sam says.

"I love my job. Love the kids. Happy to be here."

"We were just talking about our high school experiences. Never had a teacher like you. I bet you liked school back when you were in it, didn't you?"

"Actually, it was a nightmare. I bounced between being bullied and being invisible. That's why I'm here, to try to keep that from happening to other vulnerable young students."

"That's very commendable," Sam says.

"Truly heroic," I say.

The teacher looks back at me to see if I'm serious and smiles even wider when she sees that I am.

"Thank you."

"It's inspiring," I say, "and I have no doubt you make a difference."

Angel is a pale, skinny, narrow girl with no hips and no breasts and a crimson hair color not found in nature.

She is quiet and shy and nervous and has a slight speech impediment that makes her a challenge to understand.

"You know why we're here?" Sam asks.

She shakes her head.

Though she doesn't act like it, Angel is eighteen—so can be interviewed without a parent present.

"Tell us about the party at Iola Landing last Saturday night," Sam says.

Though we didn't discuss it ahead of time, it's obvious to us both that Sam should take the lead and ask most of the questions.

"Nothing to tell. I didn't go."

The classroom is beige and bland with empty chalk and bulletin boards and smells faintly of feet.

"Sorry," Sam says. "Saturday before last."

"It was pretty lame. Not much to it. I left kinda early."

"Anybody go or leave with you?"

"No. Oh, I gave Amber a ride home."

"Who?"

"Amber Matthews. New girl who needed a ride."

Here five months and still the new girl.

"Why?"

"Why what?"

"Why'd she need one?"

Angel shrugs. "I think she was ready to go and her boyfriend wasn't. I'm not sure."

"Where'd you take her?"

"Well, she said to her aunt's place at the five-acre farms in Dalkeith, but she ditched me."

"Whatta you mean?"

"I stopped by the Express Lane for some Skittles and a Sprite. When I came back out she was gone."

The Express Lane is the convenience store in the middle of town at the intersection where Highway 22 dead ends into Main Street. It's on a small lot at the only traffic light in town. The back and side of the building are dark at night, though with only a few spots in front of the building a lot of people park out there.

"Where'd you park?" I ask.

"On the side. I came in from the back by the fire department on Second Street."

"What time was it?"

"Just before midnight, 'cause they were about to close."

"Anyone else around?" I ask. "Anybody in the parking lot?"

"Empty. Like the town at that time of night. Dead."

"Why didn't you call the police?" Sam asks.

"For what?"

"*For what?* Amber disappearing?"

"Are you for real?"

"What did you think happened to her?" I ask.

"Figured she just bailed. Got in with someone else— someone cooler, one of her actual friends, or that her boyfriend changed his mind, caught up to us."

"So it didn't seem all that unusual to you?" I say.

She shakes her head. "Happens all the time. Even with people I know well. 'Cept with them I can text and say what the fuck?"

"It never crossed your mind something could be wrong?" Sam asks.

"Like what? It's Wewa. No."

"How long did you wait for her?" I ask.

"A while. Even got out and looked around, thought she might be out back pukin' or something, but nothing. I waited way past the time they locked up the store and left. Always do stuff like that. Get taken advantage of. Eventually, I went home."

"And it didn't seem strange to you that she hasn't been in school this week?" Sam says.

"She hasn't? You sure?"

"You haven't noticed?"

"We're not friends. I don't really know her. We don't have the same classes. We don't hang. The first time she ever spoke to me was when she asked me for a ride."

What she is describing is typical high school. Ordinary self-involved immaturity. Of course she would think she got ditched because a cool kid came by and offered her a ride. Of course she wouldn't notice if the new girl suddenly dropped out. She's transient. It's expected.

As we are walking out of the classroom with Angel, my mind drifts back to Shane, to his poor family, to the search underway at the moment, to his friends and girlfriend. Cody had graduated, but Swolle and Megan are still in school.

"Is Megan here today?" I ask.

Angel shakes her head. "Would you come to school if you killed *your* boyfriend?"

Chapter Twenty-five

Amber's aunt who really isn't her aunt, Francis Randolph, lives in a little wooden house on a five-acre tract of land in Dalkeith.

She's a frail, wrinkled fifty-something woman with a wicked smoker's cough who looks at least twenty years older than what she is.

We reach her place by eleven in the morning and find her still in her pajamas and already smelling of booze.

"I'm not really her aunt, but I feel sorry for the child. Her mother and I were drinking buddies back in the day. What'd she do? She in trouble? Why are you looking for her?"

She's sitting on a sinking sofa with a too-loose vinyl cover on it, a small dog of indeterminable breeding in her lap.

We are sitting across from her in the dim, smoky room in old, uncomfortable chairs covered in dog hair.

She seems to be staring at me.

"You sure you're a cop, handsome?" she says. "You have kind eyes for a cop." She turns to Sam. "Got nice eyes, don't he? Intense, but nice, you know?"

"Do you know where she is?" Sam asks. "Amber."

She shrugs.

"I know the two places she was always threatening to go to," she says. "Every time I asked for her help around here or expected her to follow a few simple rules or show some common courtesy and respect for her elders . . . she threatened to go back to her dad's or go live at Taunton's."

By *Taunton's* she means the Taunton Family Children's Home in Honeyville, a privately owned home for kids operated by a former judge and his wife, David and Abigail Taunton.

"You don't know where she is?" Sam asks.

She shakes her head. "Not for sure. Always came and went as she pleased. What has she done? Why are you looking for her?"

"When's the last time you saw her?" I ask.

"Last Saturday. I forbade her from going to a party and she went anyway. I told her if she did, not to come back, but . . . I have said that before and she has always come back before. This is the longest time she's stayed away since she showed up here at Christmas."

"What was she wearing when you last saw her?" Sam asks.

She describes the outfit and jewelry Amber was wearing in the Facebook photos and on the phones of the kids at the party in surprising detail.

"Now," she says, "I'm not going to answer any more questions until you tell me what this is about."

"I'm very sorry to have to inform you of this," Sam says, "but we've found the body of a white female in the river that we believe may be that of your . . . of Amber."

"In the river? But Amber's a good swimmer. Had she been drinking? Oh no, it . . . it can't be her. Oh my merciful Jesus. Please not that poor child. Hasn't she suffered enough?"

"**N**o one was ever going to put out an Amber Alert for Amber, were they?" I say.

We are walking back toward my car, dusting the dog hair off of us and trying to air the smoke out of our hair, clothes, and lungs.

"Wonder how long it would've taken anyone to realize she was missing if we hadn't found her?" Sam says.

"And we wouldn't have found her if we hadn't been looking for Shane," I say, shaking my head. "God, I hope we find him soon."

She nods. "Me too."

I start to say something else, but both of our phones ring.

I step away from her so we can both take our calls simultaneously.

Mine is from Merrill, my best friend and former co-worker at PCI .

"Had enough, John," he says. "Finally had enough."

"Of?"

"Us gettin' killed in the streets," he says.

I know what he's referring to. Another unarmed black man was shot and killed by the police last night. It was the second in less than a week caught on video by a nearby witness.

"Me too."

"No more sitting by watching it happen for me," he says. "Time to join the fray."

"What're you doing right now?" I ask.

138

"Just turned in my notice," he says.

"So you're free?"

"In so many ways."

"Can you meet for lunch?"

"I'll drive over," he says. "Least I can do. Your ass has two jobs and mine ain't even got one no more."

"See you at Mitchell's in half an hour," I say, and disconnect the call.

"That was Reggie," Sam says when she gets in the car.

My call ended sooner than Sam's so I have the car nice and cool by the time she gets in.

"She spoke to Amber's dad. Says he hasn't heard from her in quite a while, thought she was still with Francis, had no idea she was even missing."

I nod as I back out of Francis Randolph's little dirt driveway.

"It's a good thing Reggie interviewed him and not me," she says.

"Why's that?"

"She said he indicated it was her own fault, that he suggested that the reason she was killed was because she wasn't living in his house following his rules and obeying her stepmother. I'd'a had to bitch slap the shit out of him."

"Then I wish we'd've interviewed him."

"And missed out on the whole Francis Randolph experience?" she says. "Can you imagine talking like that about your own daughter? What a . . . We've got to find her killer and get some sort of justice for her."

"We will."

"We've got to care enough not to stop, because no
139

one else does."
    "We do."

Chapter Twenty-six

Merrick and Reggie are heading toward the No Name Café in downtown Port St. Joe in his car.

It's a rare thing that they get to have lunch together, but after sitting in on Rain's interview, he stayed down here to work on a story about how the BP Deep Horizon oil spill settlement money is being spent in Gulf County and asked if Reggie could get away.

Barbara Radcliff, the owner and operator of the No Name Café and bookstore, is a friend of theirs and always whips them up something special, plus they get to browse through the bookshelves while they wait for their food.

"What's wrong?" Merrick asks.

"I was trying to hide it," she says.

"Well you shouldn't. Not from me."

"I just feel so fuckin' bad about how I handled the Rain-Amber thing," she says.

"What could you have done differently?" he says.

"I didn't just jeopardize the investigation and the prosecution's eventual case," she says. "I lost the respect and trust of John and Sam. They handled it all very professionally but I can tell they don't look at me the same way. I wouldn't be surprised if John quits and Sam reports me."

"They probably understand better than you think. Especially John. You see the way he looks at his little girls. Besides, you'll have the opportunity to win their trust back again countless times."

"I don't know what else I could've done," she says. "I knew he didn't do it, but I can't not think like a mom, can't not protect my family."

He nods.

"I'm just already so compromised from the last big case. I feel so corrupt about what I did on it that . . . I . . . I'm not sure I should be sheriff."

"You're a great sheriff."

"I'm corrupt and compromised—the very things the previous one was. But . . . I was so proud of Rain. So proud. How he handled himself. And his commitment to not driving after he'd been drinking—even when—*especially* when being pressured by his girlfriend."

"He's a good kid."

"And it makes me so happy that he chose you to sit in with him in the interview," she says. "I mean, that's huge."

"Made me pretty happy too," he says. "Made me feel like we're a family."

"We are," she says. "That's exactly what we are."

As they're getting out at the No Name, Tim Munn, the manager at Dockside Seafood, is walking up.

"I was just about to call you," Reggie says.

"Oh yeah?" he says.

He's wearing what Reggie has come to think of as his uniform—cargo shorts, a green short-sleeved button-up fishing shirt, and a burgundy baseball camp with an FSU emblem on it.

"What're you doing *here*?" she asks. "Shouldn't you be running your own restaurant?"

"My day off," he says. "Out getting tacos and reading material. Just left Pepper's so I'm full of tacos, and now I'm stopping by here because Barbara got in the new book by my favorite author. Why do I feel like I'm being interrogated?"

"She has that effect on people," Merrick says.

"You're certainly answering like you're being interrogated," she says. "Thought you only gave those kind of detailed answers when someone's husband's askin'."

"Funny," he says, flashing a half smile on his sun-reddened face that says it really isn't.

"I need to talk to a young man who I believe works for you," she says.

"Who's that?"

"Furnell Gant."

Tim starts smiling. "He's a cook. Should be at work right now."

"What is it?"

"Last time he was arrested," he says. "Police came to the restaurant, cuffed him right there in the kitchen, and as they were dragging him out he was yelling back over his shoulder would he still have his job when he got out."

"So the sheriff's significant other is your best friend?" Sam asks.

"No. I'm just getting to know him."

"I thought you said he was. Who are you meeting for lunch?"

"Merrill, not Merrick."

143

"Oh. Who is Merrill again?"

"Merrill Monroe. My best friend since childhood. Big, badass black correctional officer. Not to be confused with Merrick McKnight. An average-sized white reporter and main squeeze of Sheriff Reggie Summers."

"Makes a lot more sense now."

I meet Merrill at the Corner Café in Wewa—a place we call Mitchell's because our friend Mitchell Johnson owns it.

An African-American man in his sixties, Mitchell operates the Corner Café in a building on Main Street that has been, among other things, a drugstore and a storefront church. He owns it and the small building next to it that was a Whites Only game room he was kept out of as a kid.

While I'm here seeing Merrill, Sam takes my car to check the Express Lane for surveillance footage and to see if the clerk working the night Amber disappeared remembers anything.

Merrill is waiting for me when I arrive and we embrace in the sort of half-hug way that includes a couple of fist pounds on the back.

Merrill Monroe, my closest friend for nearly my entire life, is a muscular black man with broad shoulders and intense, intelligent, penetrating black eyes.

Having come straight from the prison where he'd just resigned, he's still wearing his correctional officer uniform, and it's strange to think this may be the last time I ever see him in it.

As we decide what we want and wait in line, I can hear four different conversations going on around us about Shane's disappearance and Amber's crucifixion. Shocked, confused, fearful, the entire town is talking. Theorizing. Speculating. Gossiping.

We place our order at the counter, but instead of sitting there like we normally do, we find a booth in a quiet corner so we can talk privately.

"You okay?" I say.

His eyes are wide and a bit wild, and something about my familiar friend seems foreign and unfamiliar.

He nods. "In the way you askin', yeah."

"What way is that?"

"In the 'have I lost my mind 'cause I quit my job' way."

I smile.

"Ain't sayin' I know what I'm doin'," he says. "Just sayin' I know what I'm *not*. And I'm *not* gonna sit by anymore while unarmed black men and boys are being gunned down in the streets. And I'm *not* gonna be part of the prison industrial complex. I've reached my limit. A tipping point. I can't do it another second."

I nod and listen and think about how much I admire and respect him.

"The whole world is a fuckin' tinderbox right now," he says. "Got to do all I can to make sure the whole thing doesn't go up in flames."

He's right. Everywhere we turn there's cause for great alarm—the rising tide of terrorism, the proliferation of world-destroying weapons, overpopulation and the poisoning and plundering of the planet, the militant ignorance and anti-intelligence movement, the political polarization and paralysis, the mass shootings, the mass hysteria, the palpable fear and paranoia of people who feel powerless arming themselves to fight the wrong wars, cops killing unarmed citizens.

"I've had all I can take," he says.

"What're you gonna do?" I ask.

He shrugs. "Something. Join the frontline somehow, in some . . . constructive way. Don't know exactly how or what yet. Just know I have to make a positive contribution now. Right the fuck now."

I nod.

"You think I've lost my got-damn mind, don't you?"

"You know better than that," I say.

"I may actually be insane," he says. "I wouldn't know if I was, would I?"

"The world's insane," I say. "What you're saying sounds like sanity to me."

"I feel more free than at any time in my entire life," he says.

"What was it that Camus said? 'The only way to deal with an unfree world is to become so absolutely free that your very existence is an act of rebellion.'"

"I like that," he says. "That's what I'm going for." Then in his best Mookie from Spike Lee's *Do the Right Thing* he adds, "Want to be like M-M-M-Malcolm and M-M-M-Martin."

I smile and think back to the two of us watching it on VHS in my little apartment in Atlanta back when it first came out in 1989.

"You know what the man said," I say. "'The ultimate measure of a man is not where he stands in moments of comfort and convenience, but where he stands at times of challenge and controversy.'"

"Martin or Malcolm?"

"Martin," I say. "I'd be hard pressed to come up with

a quote by X off the top of my head. The point is—you measure up, man."

"Ain't done nothin' yet," he says.

"Sure you have. You've taken the first step. And it's the most critical and the most difficult. Think about how many people are seeing what's going on, see actual video footage of it and want to do something, but don't."

Mitchell walks up with our food and asks what we're talking about.

I tell him.

"I've been prayin' about what I can do," he says. "You let me know how I can help, how I can get involved. March. Sit-in. Mentoring. Whatever I can do. And today's lunch is on me."

Chapter Twenty-seven

"No security footage," Sam says when I get in the car. "Lasts a little less than a week then is erased to make room for current recordings."

She has parked my Impala on the side of Mitchell's building, left it running, the AC blasting, and is waiting for me in the passenger seat.

"Didn't figure there would be," I say. "The clerk remember seeing anything?"

"The one working now wasn't the one working that night, but I got her number and called her."

"And?"

"She can't be certain it was that night, but she thinks it was. She remembers Angel coming right before she closed and thinks it was the same night. She saw a white delivery truck pull out of the parking lot. Stood out because she had seen it riding around town earlier in the evening. Said it was plain white, big and boxy. Hasn't seen it in town since."

"That fits, doesn't it? Vehicle like that would give him the room he needs for his tools and props and—hell, he may even do what he does to them inside the back of the truck. Like a mobile murder room."

"Sounds as though it'd be big enough," she says.

"This could be our first big break. If it is him and he's—"

My phone rings. It's Susan.

"I need to take this. Sorry."

I step out of the car and take the call, walking around to the front of Mitchell's and down the sidewalk.

"What the *fuck* are you doing?" she says.

"What?"

"You didn't think I'd already know? We have friends in the courthouse. *A restraining order? Really?* The *fuck* are you thinkin'?"

"I'm thinking I don't want to lose my daughter again," I say. "I'm thinking the last time we spoke you seemed pretty cavalier about me being in her life."

"I did not," she says. "Or I didn't mean to be. But even if I came off that way . . . a restraining order? Seriously?"

"It's just to keep you from moving until paternity can be established and we can have a custody hearing."

"We need to meet and discuss this before it gets out of hand," she says.

"Okay."

"Halfway?" she says. "In Bristol at the Apalachee. Seven my time tonight?"

Crossing the river changes the time zone. She is an hour ahead of me.

"Bring Johanna," I say.

I disconnect the call, tap in Anna's number, and tell her what just happened.

"I'm not even back from Tallahassee yet and she already knows," she says. "Do you have any idea how unethical it is for someone at the courthouse to tell her like that?"

"She wants to meet to discuss it," I say. "Think maybe it scared her. Sounded like she's open to working it out."

"I don't trust her. Be very careful where she's concerned."

"I will," I say. "Have too much to lose not to."

This time when I get back in the car, Sam is on the phone.

"Sorry about that," I say when she ends her call.

"No problem. That was Reggie. She just finished interviewing Furnell Gant. Said we can interview him if we want to but that she's convinced enough to clear him. He was there to see a particular girl. Didn't even know who Amber and Angel were. He gave a couple of kids a ride to another party back in St. Joe later that night. Has solid alibis nearly all night."

I nod. "Didn't think it was him," I say. "We're looking for someone older and white, not a high school kid still living at home with his parents."

"Agreed."

I put the car in gear and back out of the small Corner Café parking lot.

"I told her about the white delivery truck," she says. "She's gonna see if she can find a match in any of the databases for a similar truck used in any crimes and get a list of the ones registered in the area."

I take a right on Second Street and a left on Lake Grove Road.

"I think if it's him," Sam says, "I mean if the truck is his . . . I think it's a very good chance he's mobile and was just passing through."

I nod. "Would explain why search and rescue haven't found any more victims in the river. If he was using it as some sort of killing field or dumping ground . . . think

150

they'd've found more already."

"Probably, but . . . the river only begrudgingly gives up its bodies. Look at Shane."

I frown and nod and think again about Tommy and Michelle.

"But," I say, "if we we're saying the killer was just passing through, that Amber was just random, convenient, available—I don't know. I have a hard time buying that. It's not like he's cruising around in his mobile killing machine and sees a car with a young girl sitting in it and stops in and grabs her, not knowing how long whoever was with her was going to be in the store."

"Well, when you put it like that . . ." she says. "The truck may not even belong to the killer. Even if it does, the mobile killing machine thing is just an idea, a theory, but . . . what if we're right about that and right about him passing through? Maybe it wasn't purely random, not purely opportunistic. What if he stalked her, followed her for a while? The clerk said she had seen the vehicle in town earlier."

"That makes more sense. Then we have to figure out what brought him to town—if he doesn't live here—and where and how Amber crossed his path."

"What if Shane saw something or the killer thought he saw something and that's what got him killed?" she asks.

"But Shane wasn't around—and hadn't been. He got into town a week after she was killed."

She nods. "They're most likely not connected. Just trying to consider all the possibilities."

"Which is good," I say. "Like you said, all we have are ideas and theories. Have to keep thinking, talking, figuring as we keep uncovering more information."

"Glad you feel like that," she says. "'Cause I have

another. I've been hesitant to say it to you, but . . ."

"Why?"

"Because of Reggie, but . . . Anyway, what if we moved off her son too quick? We said he's too young and lacks the sophistication for something like this, that it's far more likely a practiced serial, but . . . since we haven't found any other bodies, any other evidence that there is a serial at work . . . what if Rain read up on some sick shit or saw a movie or something . . . and . . . tried to make it look like . . . I don't know . . . something that it wasn't?"

"It's crossed my mind," I say. "I think it's highly unlikely, but you're right, we shouldn't rule it out. Let's keep it as a possibility as we continue to gather evidence and information."

Less than a mile back from the landing at the end of the road where the search for Shane and other victims continues, we veer off to the left and drive to Iola Landing.

Chapter Twenty-eight

Iola was once a thriving small town, the place where the railroad met the river, where goods were loaded and unloaded, shipped and hauled, bought and sold.

Now nothing remains of the little town, and the only evidence that the railroad ran this way is a huge round, bowl-shaped indentation in the ground near the landing where the old railway turntable once sat. Turntables or wheelhouses were used for turning railroad rolling stock, in this case the locomotive, which, when it reached the river, had to be turned so it could then push the train back to Port St. Joe and the ships in St. Joseph Bay.

We park at the landing not far from the cement boat launch that slopes down to the river below.

It takes a little while, but eventually we find the remnants of the bonfire where the kids gather to drink and talk and socialize and hook up. It's back in the woods a bit from the landing, but only fifty feet or so, in a small clearing surrounded by oak and pine and cypress trees.

The area is littered with beer bottles and cigarette butts and a variety of trash, the charred logs in the center of it all dusted with and surrounded by thick gray ash.

"Chances are we're not gonna find anything here," I say. "Most likely nothing to find. But I wanted to at least take a look around."

She nods. "Unless it was one of the kids from the party, he wasn't here. An older guy would stand out like a mofo at a gathering like this one."

"Unless he was hidden," I say.

"A watcher in the woods," she says, her eyes widening, her voice rising. "Could be. Especially if he stalked her for a while."

"What if he wasn't stalking *her* so much as the party. He comes here looking for prey—maybe even picks out a few possibilities—but when she leaves with Angel, she becomes his target. Or they both do. But she's the one left alone in the dark parking lot so he takes her."

She shrugs. "Far more likely he already has his eye on her, that something about her fuels his fantasy, that she is specifically and not randomly his choice."

I nod. "You're right. That fits the profile of these kinds of killers better."

"So," she says. "You want to split up and look around for a while, or see if Reggie will assign some deputies to do it?"

"I'd rather us do it—at least at first. At least for a little while."

"Let's do it," she says.

And we do.

We search in concentric circles, starting at the fire and working our way out ever wider, her covering one half, me covering the other.

The May day is pleasant, the early afternoon sun balanced by the breeze blowing in off the river. Above us branches wave ever so slightly in the wind, the Spanish moss draped over them swaying lazily.

I think about Merrill again and all he's doing, and wonder if I'm doing enough.

I'm trying to figure out what else I might do when Sam begins to yell for me.

"What is it?" I say, moving in her direction.

She is over about forty feet or so on the backside of the woods opposite the river, her small frame completely eclipsed by the magnolia tree she's behind.

"He was here," she yells. "He was right fuckin' here."

I rush over to her, careful not to touch or step on anything on the backside of the tree where she's staring.

"We were right. He was stalking her. He stood right here and looked right through there and watched her. So it's probably not Rain."

I turn back to look in the direction she's pointing.

From where she's standing, just above the under-brush and between the trees, there's a perfect line of sight to where the kids would've been hanging out around the fire.

"Look at this," she says. "Look."

I turn and take a few steps, then come up behind her and look over the top of her head at the carving in the tree.

The cuts and carvings in the tree are crude but there can be no doubt what they form—a nude female figure crucified face down on a cross, her legs spread slightly to accommodate a phallic-shaped piece of pipe penetrating her.

Chapter Twenty-nine

While Sam waits at Iola Landing for forensics to arrive, I drive to the end of the road to check in with Ralph and Tommy.

I find Ralph first.

"How's it going?" I ask.

"It's a goin'," he says. "Slow and steady. All it takes is time and stubbornness, and we have plenty of both."

"What's the longest it has taken to find someone?" I ask.

"Thirty-two days."

"Wow."

"Bodies do tricky things down there on the bottom. We call it walkin'. Can go on for miles, just bouncing along."

"What's the shortest?"

"Less than an hour."

I nod and look out at the activity on the river, the slow-moving boats and the search and rescue volunteers aboard them.

"But we always get our man," he says. "Or woman. We won't leave until we do."

I nod. "What y'all do for our community, and for the

families of the victims, is such a gift. Thank you again."

"Our pleasure."

"Have you seen Tommy?"

"He's around here somewhere. Only goes home for a few hours in the middle of the night. Rest of the time he's here searching, helping, supporting. Just stand there and act like you need help and he'll show up eventually."

Unable to find Tommy, I walk over to the first house on Byrd Parker Drive and knock on the door.

The first two houses back up to the river and have great views of the dock. Reggie was supposed to have sent someone to interview the occupants, but it won't hurt for me to do it too.

The gruff old man who answers the door at the first house informs me that he and his wife were at the Tupelo Festival until after dark and didn't see anything. He also asks when we'll wrap up all the commotion at the landing and quit bothering them.

The elderly lady in glasses who answers the door at the second home tells me her name is Vera and invites me in and offers me lemonade.

"This is very good lemonade," I say.

"It's sort of my speciality."

She is tall and thin and frail, her voice soft and airy.

"You know what happened here on Saturday?" I ask. "Know why search and rescue has set up near your home and is dragging the river?"

She nods. "I saw the poor dear go under."

"You did?"

"Sure did."

"Has anyone talked to you about it?"

"Not yet, but I called the substation this morning and told the sweet girl who answered the phone what I saw. She said they'd send someone out to take my statement. Are you that someone?"

"I surely am."

I make a show of digging out the pen and small notebook from my pocket and turning on my recorder.

"Where were you and what were you doing when you witnessed what happened?" I ask.

"I was . . . I was watching a movie on the television, on one of those stations that plays the old ones that I like so much. Most of them I saw in the theater when they first came out. But that was a long time ago. A commercial came on and I got up to get a glass of water. I stepped over to my sliding glass door and looked out. I always do that. Every time I get up. Why have such a beautiful view if you don't look at it every chance you get? Anyway, I was looking across the way when a scream caught my attention and I looked over at the dock."

"A scream?"

"Not like in distress. Like playful. More of a yell, I guess."

"What'd you see when you looked over?"

"A young man in the water. I'm assuming he's the poor dear who's missing. He had a military haircut. He was treading water. He looked tired and like maybe he was having a hard time staying up. Next to him there was a girl on one of those wave runner things. I'm watching, thinking he needs to get on that thing with her or climb up on the dock. Next thing I know she takes off and he gets snatched under the water."

"Snatched?"

"Yes."

"Like he was pulled?"

"I guess. At the time I didn't think much of it. Young man like him. Strong. Fit. I figured he'd come right back up. I feel so ashamed now, but it didn't occur to me then that something could really be wrong. I mean, I was curious. I actually stepped back over here to get my binoculars, but then my movie came back on and I got into it. I told myself I'd go look again during the next commercial—they have so blame many of them. But then by the next one I had to go to the little girls' room. By the next break I was asleep and . . . to be honest, I didn't think about it again until I saw it on the news yesterday. Did I . . . Am I the reason . . . he wasn't . . . that he died?"

"No ma'am, you're not, but what you're doing now is a tremendous help to us. You're sure he didn't just go under? He was pulled?"

"That's what it looked like to me."

Walking back toward the landing, I call Reggie and tell her what Vera her next door neighbor had said.

"I was gonna go by there on my way home this evening," she says. "I'm glad you spoke to her."

"How well do you know her?" I ask. "How reliable is she?"

"Don't know her very well at all, sad to say. I went over and met her when we first moved here. Took her a little Christmas gift during the holidays, but that's about it. But if she's right, we're talking a gator, right?"

"Seems most likely," I say, "but . . ."

"But what?"

"It's probably a gator," I say. "But, and I know this is farfetched, someone could have pulled him under."

"That is farfetched but you're right, it's at least a possible if not likely scenario based on what she saw."

"Or," I say.

"Yeah?"

"Think about the timing of it," I say. "Megan takes off and he goes under. What if his foot got caught in the bowline of the Jet Ski somehow and it yanked him under when she took off?"

"Oh my God," she says.

"Can you have the techs check the tie rope on the Jet Ski to see if—"

"I'll call you back."

Chapter Thirty

"You still looking for Tommy?" Ralph says.

I tell him I am. I have just walked back over to the landing from Vera's and am still juiced by what she told me.

"He's on the other side of the river, searching the woods behind the houseboat. You want a ride over there?"

"Thanks."

On the ride across the river in one of Ralph's search and rescue boats, I realize just how long a swim it was for Shane and Cody. It's hard to imagine this long, exhausting swim didn't contribute to what happened to Shane, and maybe it did, but if Vera is right and he was snatched under, it may not have had any impact at all.

Of course, it could be that when he was pulled under he lacked the strength and energy to break free and resurface.

Before we reach the other side, I call Sam and let her know what's going on. She tells me she's still waiting for the crime scene techs to arrive and will get a ride back to her car with them then head home for the night.

Ralph steers the bow of the boat up next to the houseboat and I jump onto the porch and then from the porch to the bank beyond.

I find Tommy up a small path filled with animal tracks near where the owner of the houseboat has his generator chained to a tree.

"John?"

He's happy and a little surprised to see me at first but then grows alarmed.

"Did they send you to—"

"No. Sorry. I just came to check on you."

"Oh, okay. Thanks, man."

He takes a few steps back down the trail and we embrace.

"How are you?" I ask.

I know it's a stupid question, but it's the only one I've got.

"I'm okay. Mostly just sad and tired."

I nod and look around.

"They won't let me on the water," he says. "Don't want me seeing him when they pull him in, so . . . I'm searching everywhere else I can. Every bank I can find, up onto the hill. I searched the houseboat—inside and out, all around it. I've walked all over the woods. Searched all the exposed roots of the cypress trees along the banks. They don't want me to, don't want me to see him after he's been . . . in the water this long, and I don't want to either, but . . . at this point I just want to find him."

"I understand. But they will find him. Ralph says they've never not found someone. And they won't quit until they do."

He nods. "Told me the same thing. And I get it. 'Course they weren't even in existence when his brother went missing. He's never been found. I . . . I just . . . need to do something. But I'm starting to think I need to do

162

something else."

"Why's that?"

"Starting to have crazy thoughts, man," he says.

"Like what? Are you okay?"

"Like thinking someone killed him. There were footprints on this little path and I thought what if someone snuck in from over here, swam over there and killed him?"

"Why would you think that?"

"I don't know. Just random, crazy stuff. I see footprints and I think stuff like that. I searched the houseboat because I pictured him being dazed and floating over here and climbing in and lying down and passing out or wandering in the woods."

"It's all normal thoughts," I say. "It's shock and grief and fatigue and dehydration and lack of sleep."

"I know, but the footprints are of bare feet."

I nod, feeling overwhelming compassion for him. The footprints are probably those of the houseboat owner walking up to put gas in his generator, but I can understand the leaps of absurdity and futile hope they engender.

"I've been thinking," he says. "I'm gonna take a little ride up to Fort Benning and tell his friends and talk to them about him. Think it would be cathartic. I know it would do me some good. I was wondering if you'd consider going with me?"

I didn't have time, couldn't get away, had far too many responsibilities with two investigations and my chaplaincy duties and my new family responsibilities, but how could I refuse him anything?

"Of course," I say. "Of course I will. It'd be my honor."

Chapter Thirty-one

I find myself with a few extra minutes before having to leave to meet Susan, and decide to stop by to see Megan Stripling on my way out of town.

The Striplings live in a small wooden house in Blue Gator, not far from the Jehu Cemetery.

There are no cars in the drive and there doesn't look to be anyone at home.

After a long while of knocking, the door opens a fraction and Megan peeks out of the darkness behind it.

"You here by yourself?" I ask.

"Yes, sir."

I'm here more out of concern for her than anything else, more as a minister than a detective, but since she's such a young girl at home alone, I press the record button on the digital recorder in my pocket in case our interaction is ever called into question.

"Would you step out here on the porch and talk to me for just a minute?"

She slowly opens the door the rest of the way and sort of slinks out onto the porch in wrinkled pajamas. Her hair is matted and her face is puffy.

"I just wanted to check on you," I say. "They said

you weren't at school today."

She doesn't respond.

She has yet to make eye contact with me. Her unfocused eyes just drift about as her head bobbles about slightly.

"Megan?"

She stops moving her head but still doesn't look at me.

"Megan," I say louder.

Her eyes sort of swim over in my direction.

"Did you take something? What did you take?"

"I'm not on . . . I haven't taken anything. I . . . just . . . I'm fuckin' sad, okay? So fuckin' sad."

"Is that why you weren't at school today?"

"Nobody understands," she says. "I loved Shane. I *love* Shane. Still. I'll never stop loving him. Not ever. And now . . . he's gone . . . and I'm all alone. All alone. And everybody thinks I killed him. I didn't kill him. I loved him. I could never hurt him. Never. I'd die for him. I'd give my life right now to bring him back if I could. I'd rather him live than me."

"I'm gonna find out what happened to him," I say. "If you didn't do it I'll make sure everyone knows. Okay? Just hold on a little longer. Be strong for him. Would you like to talk to someone? I can recommend a good counselor who can help."

A horn honks as her mother races into the yard, slams on her breaks, slides to a stop, and jumps out.

"Megan, get inside," she yells. "And you, you get the fuck out of my yard."

Megan looks genuinely afraid and begins to stumble back inside.

Handing her my card, I say, "I'm here if you want to talk. If not me, talk to somebody."

"Hasn't she been through enough?" her mom says to me. "Not enough that she loses her boyfriend, but y'all make everyone think she killed him."

"We haven't said or done anything that would indicate that," I say.

"Bullshit. Just go. And don't come back without a warrant. And don't question my child again without her attorney. Understand?"

"Ma'am, listen to me. I stopped by because I was worried about her. I was concerned when she wasn't in school today. She's depressed and in shock and shouldn't be left alone right now. She should also talk to a counselor who can—"

"Who the fuck do you think you are? Don't tell me how to raise my own goddamn child. Do you hear me? Now go. Now."

She rushes past me, up onto the porch and inside the door, and slams it behind her.

Back in the car I call Reggie.

"I'm worried about Megan Stripling," I say. "Seems as though the court of small-town public opinion has already convicted her."

"I've heard that's what's being said. Lot of people posting about it on Facebook too."

"Would you consider making a statement that stresses that we don't have a suspect yet, that we don't know that it's anything other than an accidental drowning at this point, then reach out to her and get a counselor to see her?"

"Are you sure?"

"I am."

"What if she turns out to have had something to do with what happened to Shane?"

"Then we will still have acted humanely and with compassion, which is the least we can do in any circumstance and situation."

"Think you may be getting your two jobs mixed up," she says.

"I might be, but would that be such a bad thing?"

Chapter Thirty-two

"You mind if we eat while we talk?" Susan asks.

I shake my head. "Of course not."

We are in a booth in the back of the Apalachee in Bristol. The old seafood restaurant, a fixture in this area for as long as I can remember, is mostly empty. Johanna and I are on one side, Susan on the other.

Partly because of Susan's erratic behavior, partly because it's a habit formed from most of my investigative interactions these days, I have the mall digital recorder in my pocket recording our conversation.

I had no way of knowing which Susan I would get, but I didn't expect this one—warm, friendly, calm.

Johanna's in my lap and I find myself unable to stop kissing her head.

"Your hair smells so good," I say.

She is concentrating on coloring the picture on the table in front of her, but says a soft "Thank you, Daddy."

Susan smiles at us.

Who are you?

She is so different in nearly every way from the last time I saw her that she seems not the same person at all.

"This is what I always wanted for us," she says.

The waitress comes and Susan orders—for all of us, presuming to know what I would want.

She doesn't get it right but I don't contradict her.

"Sorry again that the filings caught you off guard," I say. "Just knew I had to prove paternity and petition for a custody hearing and just wanted you to be here so I could."

She nods. "I get it. You love your daughter. You're just trying to make sure you are in her life."

I nod.

"The thing is . . . the way you are with her—" tears glisten in her eyes "—is . . . that's what . . . that's the way . . . I've always wished my dad was with me."

I am overcome with sadness for her. Images of her trying to get her dad's approval and attention over the years flash in my mind.

"I can't keep her from having that, can't deny her the thing I've most wanted my whole life."

Johanna stops coloring and looks up.

"Mommy's okay," Susan says. "Just sort of happy and sad at the same time."

I hug Johanna and lean over and kiss her on the cheek.

She kisses me back then climbs down, walks over, climbs up into Susan's lap and hugs her.

It's such a perfect act of kindness that it hurts my heart with happiness, and though I want to make sure she never feels like she has to take care of Susan, I also want her always to be moved with compassion for the pain of others.

"You're such a sweet girl," Susan says, "but Mommy is fine. Mommy is mostly happy. Okay?"

"Okay, Mommy," she says. "But I'm gonna stay over

here with you for a while."

What Susan does next gives me more genuine hope for us, for Johanna, than anything in a long time.

"Hey, Mommy is really good. Okay? And Daddy doesn't get to see you nearly as much as he wants to. I really think you should sit with him every chance you get."

Johanna looks across the table at me.

"You miss me a lot, don't you Daddy?" she says.

"All the time, baby girl. All the time."

"Since Mommy's okay, I'll sit with you, okay?"

"Okay."

Our food comes and I begin to cut up Johanna's chicken strips to let them cool.

"You wanna say a blessing, Daddy, or do you want me to?"

"You," I say. "You do such good blessings."

She folds her small hands and bows her little head and says, "Thank you for the food . . . and the flowers . . . and the sky . . . and Mommy and Daddy. Amen."

"Amen," Susan and I say in unison.

We eat in comfortable silence.

After we finish and Johanna is coloring again, Susan says, "We can work this out. On our own. We don't need the court to get involved."

"Okay."

"You don't have to prove paternity," she says. "You're on the birth certificate. You've been getting regular visits and paying child support. All we have to do is figure out a visitation schedule we can agree on."

"A way to co-parent," I say. "And to stick with it."

"Yes."

"I want us to make all decisions jointly. All the big

ones at least."

"Okay."

"I want more time," I say. "I don't want it to be disruptive, but I think we can do it in a way that isn't."

"I know we can. And we will. But, John, listen to what I want. Okay? Really hear me. I want to move back to Atlanta. I can't live with my parents one more minute."

"But—"

"Let me finish. Listen to me now, I've given this a lot of careful thought. Here's what I propose. You two Skype every single day. You have her most of the summer and most all of any long school breaks. Between now and the fall when she starts kindergarten, we do a week at a time. When she starts kindergarten . . . we do every other weekend, but . . . listen to this . . . the school I want us to put her in is only Monday through Thursday. On your weekends, we meet Thursday and Sunday evenings. That way you get Thursday night, Friday, Friday night, Saturday, Saturday night, and most of the day Sunday. What do you think?"

I can't help but smile. "I think it's a very reasonable and generous proposal. And I really think it can work. But I have two concerns. I don't want this to be too much on her, too disruptive in her little life."

"I don't think it will be," she says.

"I'll want to come up and see her up there. Go to important school events and programs she's in. As she gets older, I'll want us to be flexible on which weekends she comes down for because I won't want her to miss important social functions with her friends. And occasionally I'll want her to bring a friend or two with her. This will work if we both put her first, truly work together to do what's best for her."

171

"I agree. And we will. We both love her more than anything. We will do that. I will do it. I promise."

"But this past weekend you just showed up and changed everything and took her back early and—"

"I'm sorry about that. That was a . . . It was a bad time . . . I won't do that again."

"We need a legally binding custody or shared-time agreement—as I think they call it now—filed with and approved by the court."

She nods. "I know. I know you have every right to not trust me. So . . . here's what I was thinking."

She removes a file folder from the booth beside her and hands it to me.

"Here's a signed and notarized affidavit saying you are her father and me agreeing to everything I've just said. You can have Anna draw up the actual custody agreement and file it, but this will serve as some insurance for you in the meantime. And to show even more good faith, if we're going to do a week at a time, yours can start tonight. I've packed her up and brought all her things with us so she can go back with you now. I'll leave for Atlanta tonight. I'll go up, get settled in, and be ready for her by the end of the week."

She looks at Johanna. "You're excited about going home with Daddy tonight, aren't you?"

Johanna nods but continues to concentrate on her coloring.

"Why?" I ask. "Why the change? Why are you doing all this?"

"Because," she says, "if anything ever happens to me, I don't want my parents getting her."

Chapter Thirty-three

When Johanna and I get home, I find Tommy and Michelle and Anna on our back porch looking at the moon reflecting on Julia and drinking wine.

Johanna is asleep, her head on my shoulder, as I carry her in.

I haven't been able to call Anna because my phone died. Her eyes widen. "Wow. Either it went wildly better than I ever could've imagined or you finally snapped, killed Susan, and took Johanna."

"Thankfully the former."

"Oh, John," she says. "That makes me so happy. I just hope it will last."

"It will. I'll explain later.

"We're so happy for you, John," Tommy says.

"Hope you don't mind that we're here," Michelle says. "It's the only way I could get him to leave for a little while."

"Of course not. I'm glad y'all are. Let me put her down. I'll be right back."

A short while later, when I return to the back porch from putting Johanna down and checking on Taylor, Tommy is crying.

"When Mom and Dad died, I swore to myself and

God I would always protect and take care of Shane," he says. "I've always been so protective over him."

"Overprotective," Michelle says.

He smiles through his tears. "Yes. Overprotective. It's funny . . . I really didn't want him going into the army. Especially the Rangers, but . . . well, Dad had been in the army. Always wanted us to go in. Shane told him he was going to do it before Dad died. That's the only reason I agreed to it, the only reason I supported it. And he was so good at it. So strong and fast and tough. An ideal soldier. Still, I worried about him every single day. Prayed for him every single night. I thought if anything ever happened to him, at least it would be while he was doing what he wanted to do, what he had promised Dad he would. But this? A stupid swimming accident. I . . . I can't . . . I'm not . . . This isn't how it's supposed to be. What a waste. What a senseless, tragic waste. I just . . . can't . . ."

Michelle stands and steps over to him, sitting on the arm of the old wooden chair, leaning over to hold him.

As she does, he breaks down and begins to sob.

In another moment, we are all weeping together.

"It's . . . so—" he says between sobs and snorts "—senseless, it—I haven't told anyone this . . . not even Michelle—it . . . has me . . . questioning God."

Anna and I move over to where they are. I put a hand on Tommy's shoulder while she puts her arm around Michelle.

"That's . . . the . . . real reason . . . I'm spending so much . . . time at the river. I don't know what . . . else to do. I'm . . . certainly in no shape to . . . minister to someone else."

We are all silent. It's a poignant moment, the tension

of which is broken when the old wooden chair breaks and they fall to the ground.

Neither of them are hurt and both begin to laugh, their faces a disconnect of tearful eyes and smiling mouths.

"You ever question God?" Anna asks.

We have just finished making love and are in our dark room lying on our bed, her head on my chest.

"Not in moments like these," I say.

"I'm serious."

"My whole life. My faith or practice or whatever it is . . . is just a series of questions."

"Have you ever lost faith?"

"Not like you mean," I say. "Not like Tommy meant, but only because I don't have that kind of faith."

"What kind is that?"

"I don't know . . . It's complicated. But basically it comes down to belief. I think people who think they lose their faith actually just lose their belief in certain things. Or they begin to question certain things they used to believe. In some cases, the belief is all they had, so once it's gone, there's nothing else. In other cases, getting the belief out of the way introduces them to what runs far deeper. But . . . I could be wrong—about all of it. I'm still drunk on you, your love, your body, our lovemaking."

"I feel so bad for him," she says.

"Me too. And not just him. Michelle is trying to be strong for him, but she's struggling too. I'll tell you who else is . . . Megan. She's in a very bad way."

"Harder to feel bad for the person who may have killed him."

175

"I understand, but . . ."

"I know. I know. Compassion isn't just for those who deserve it."

"Compassion is just putting yourself in her place. If she did it, she may not have meant to. Or maybe she did. Maybe she's an insecure, overwrought, overemotional teenage girl who got rejected and acted rashly and did something she wishes she could now take back."

"But she can't."

"No," I say. "She can't. Whether she did it or had anything to do with it or not. But I don't think she did anything purposefully. And maybe nothing at all. Still most likely an accidental drowning."

"So very much suffering in the world," she says.

"Most of it self-inflicted," I say. "But not all. Not nearly all."

Taylor makes a sleeping snorting sound over the monitor on Anna's bedside table.

"Wickedness and suffering and pain and monsters who rape and kill and crucify young girls and throw them in the river," Anna says. "And we've brought two tiny, sweet, precious girls into that world."

"And we'll do all we can to protect them," I say.

"But there's a limit to what we can do," she says.

"There is. And I hate it. But I suspect both Johanna and Taylor are going to introduce us to all sorts of limits we have—most of them we aren't even aware of yet."

Chapter Thirty-four

Some eighty miles away, in a bed and bedroom of their own, Samantha Michaels and Daniel Davis also lie naked— Sam on her back, Daniel on his side next to her, rubbing the scars where her breasts used to be.

Sam's already small body looks even more slight in the absence of breasts, which when added to her too-pale skin, blond hair, and light blue eyes gives her the appearance of fading away.

Too plain to be pretty, too small and straight to be womanly, too boyish to be sexy—is what most men and some women might say about her, but to Daniel Davis she is absolute perfection, the woman of his dreams, the only woman in the world so far as he's concerned.

"So tell me, Doc," she says. "What's the deal with this particular sicko?"

"No great mystery in one sense," he says. "Greatest mystery of all in another."

"Let's hear it."

"I'd rather just trace the outline of your scars and kiss your neck."

"You can do both. You've done it before."

She's so in love with him, so enjoys the gentle caress

of his fingertips on her skin. Hard to fathom now how she could have suspected him of being a serial killer when she first met him.

In her defense, serial killers are often quiet, shy, bookish, religious types, but God, she couldn't've been more wrong.

"Somewhere during his development, probably pretty early on, his concepts and constructs of sexuality and religion and suffering became intertwined in the darkest and most sadistic ways. Perhaps his particular form of neglect and abandonment and abuse was particularly sexual and religious. Perhaps it wasn't. Perhaps he arrived with an inability to form bonds with other humans. Perhaps his attempts at bonding were met with torture—emotional, psycho-sexual-religious torture. Maybe it included none of that and those components are only in the dark horrors inside his head, stored with the fantasies fueling his triggers, signatures, and trophies."

"I'm assuming that's the *no great mystery* part," she says, her voice thick and hoarse.

"Are you getting turned on again?" he asks.

"You know I love it when you talk like that to me," she says.

"About sexual sadism?" he asks, laughing.

"I love the way your mind works. Love your knowledge and wisdom. Love how tenderly you touch me when you're talking about such brutal things."

"Does that mean round two is about to commence?" he asks.

"Just as soon as you tell me about the greatest mystery of all."

"That of human evil," he says. "No matter what

happened to him as a child, no matter what sick, disgusting, horrific shit was done to him, there are thousands of people on the planet who have gone through far worse who have never intentionally harmed another human being in any way. Why does he? Why does he go to such lengths to do it? It's not unlike why is it that every child molester was molested but not everyone who was molested becomes a child molester?"

Her necklace still smells of her.

Of her soap and perfume, of her skin, of her fear. Of her blood.

He holds the tiny cord up above his upturned face so that the teardrop-shaped rose quartz hovers just above his flared nostrils.

The smell makes the bulge in his pants grow, stiffen, tighten.

He needs release. Needs to be one with her again.

Unzipping his jeans, he begins to rub roughly his erection. Pawing awkwardly at it.

Offer your bodies as living sacrifices. This is true worship.

With my body I thee worship.

Making this connection with her, *this reconnection*, is the only thing with the slightest chance of calming him right now—now after the desecration, after they had profaned his sacred sacrifice.

It wasn't just a desecration. It was an abomination of desolation. A sacrilege.

But when ye shall see the abomination of desolation, spoken of by Daniel the prophet, standing where it ought not, then let them that be in Judaea flee to the mountains.

179

His offerings were between him and God. Private. Holy. Hidden. The truest, most sincere sacrifice is the one that nobody sees. Only God.

Take heed that ye do not your righteous acts before men, to be seen of them, otherwise ye have no reward of your Father which is in heaven. When thou doest your righteous acts, let not thy left hand know what thy right hand doeth, That thine acts may be in secret, and thy Father which seeth in secret himself shall reward thee openly.

Is that what this is? Is this the beginning of him being rewarded openly? No. God wouldn't use such base and ignorant men to reward him. This is the work of the enemy, trying to destroy and humiliate him before he can finish his race and win his reward.

No one had ever before found one of his offerings. No one had known of his existence until now. Now they know. Now they'll be looking. Searching. Hunting. Hunting for him.

So Christ was sacrificed once to take away the sins of many.

They didn't understand. How could they?

His third foster mom had warned him. Hide who you are. Keep secret what you do.

He was good at keeping secrets. He had never told what was done to him, what he was made to do—with and to his sister.

He can still see her pale, undeveloped, nude little body face down on foster dad number two's huge crucifix. Handing him the smaller crucifix, telling him what to do with it. The man's stubbled, sandpaper-rough face rubbing his as he whispered in his ear with whiskey-foul breath.

My son, do not reject the discipline of the Lord or loathe his reproof, for whom the Lord loves he reproves, even as a father corrects the son in whom he delights. The body is many members. Children

180

obey your parents. Make of your bodies a living sacrifice.

The beatings. The rapes. The torture. The humiliations. The orders. The way he eventually obeyed everyone. He remembers and relives them all.

For whom the Lord loveth he chasteneth, and scourgeth every son whom he receiveth.

His sister has long since been free. How long before he will be, before his offerings will be found acceptable in the sight of God and he can join her in the true freedom of forgiveness and fellowship.

Well done, thou good and perfect servant, enter into the joy prepared for you before the foundation of the world was ever laid.

Lowering the necklace, he takes the teardrop rose quartz in his mouth, tears of his own filling his eyes as sucks on it until he achieves release.

Tension gone, temporarily satiated, he is overcome with sadness. Now when he tries to smell the necklace it will only smell like his saliva.

Need another. Another sacrifice. Another sacrament to take with him to relive his work once it is done.

Chapter Thirty-five

The next morning, bone-weary and rawboned, Tommy and I drive up through Dothan and Eufaula to Columbus to meet with Shane's friends and fellow Rangers.

They are not what I expect.

Diverse. Friendly. Funny. Kind. Caring.

All but one are far smaller and more immature than I imagined they would be, their as-yet-to-fill-out bodies swallowed up by their too-big uniforms. In many, many ways they are what they look like—children dressed up as soldiers.

Of the six boys who meet us at what was Shane's favorite place to eat, two are Hispanic, two are black, and two are white. Of the white boys, one is gay and one is muscular and macho and monosyllabic.

We meet them at a Southern soul food joint on Victory Drive just a couple of miles from base.

The place, Sweet Willy's Soul Food Station, is inside an old converted service station, the big bay doors and certain tires and tools still here. Its slogan is Fuel for the Soul.

All around the building and across the street are pawn shops, title brokers, and check-cashing and payday loan places.

The area, like much of Columbus, is run-down to the point of being nearly in ruins and in need of revitalization.

The eight of us sit at a table for ten—two places set for fallen and missing comrades, Shane and a boy from Texas named Carl who died in an Airborne accident.

A self-conscious young African-American woman takes our drink order, and Tommy begins to get the stories of the boys he doesn't know. He'd met the others at the infantry graduation and the turning blue ceremony, but not the two white guys.

"Well, I'm Jayson and I'm the gay one," one of them says.

His voice is deep and resonant and has a professional broadcasting quality to it.

"You ever done any radio work?" I say.

"A little. But I want to be the artist whose song is being played, not the DJ playing the song," he says.

"He gonna be the first openly gay country music star," Kahleel, one of the black guys, says.

"Think Luke Bryan beat him to it," Rashard, the other black guy, adds.

"I said *openly* gay."

Tommy turns to the other white guy. "I don't think we've met."

"Joshua Darden, sir," he says.

"He the buttoned-up badass one," Kahleel says.

"Nice to meet you both. Thank you all for coming. This really means a lot to me."

Our waitress returns with our drinks, which includes beer for all the boys—including Shane and Carl, and shots to toast them with.

Sweet Willy's, like a lot of joints around the base, serves alcohol to boys in uniform regardless of their age, asserting if you're old enough to serve your country, you're old enough to drink.

"To Shane and Carl," Joshua Darden says.

Everyone raises a glass—including the waitress who has brought one for herself—and toasts Shane and Carl.

"To Shane and Carl," everyone says in unison.

Tommy and I toast with sweet tea—me because I'm a recovering alcoholic, him because he's a teetotaling youth pastor—but all the boys and the waitress do a shot and a beer chaser.

As they do, I see a look pass between the waitress and Jayson that I can't quite figure out.

"Both were in the process of making fine soldiers," Joshua says, "but Shane was the best."

"You mean next to you," Orlando, one of the Hispanic boys, says.

Joshua smiles.

"Shane was the only one who could keep up with Josh," Honor, the other Hispanic boy, says. "Only one who gave him any competition at all."

Joshua nods and lifts his glass in the direction of the empty chair reserved for Shane.

"Still can't believe he's gone, man," Kahleel says. "Fuckin' . . . hell . . . Now my ass cryin' like a little bitch."

Tommy nods and puts his arm around the young man as tears begin to stream down his cheeks.

The young waitress, whose name is Kayden and who seems to know all the boys by name, comes back and takes our order.

In keeping with Sweet Willy's service station theme, her uniform is a pair of blue button-front cotton coveralls, complete with automotive patches and what looks like smears of grease.

She and Jayson are familiar and friendly, but there is also something weird passing between them.

After Jayson orders, he says, "You know what Shane would want. Maybe just give that to Carl too."

"I'm not giving Shane's special to anyone else."

"Okay. Damn. I don't know what he would want. Just give him what I ordered."

She nods, then notices I am looking at them and grows even more awkward and self-conscious. She looks back at me, eyes wide, brows raised. "Anything else?"

I shake my head. "Thanks."

"So tell me about Shane as a Ranger," Tommy says. "As your friend."

"He was a great guy," Jayson says. "Truly. You and Michelle did a wonderful job raising him."

"He never complained," Joshua says. "Always shouldered his own load. Helped out when he could. Was respected by the troops and his commanders."

"He was crazy," Kahleel says. "Knew how to have fun. Loved to dance. Danced like a brother."

"Not all he did like a brother," Orlando says.

They all laugh. Well, everyone but Josh.

"Whatta you mean?" Tommy asks.

"He liked sisters," Rashard says. "We go out and he be competition for me and Kahleel. Hell, we go to one of those country music clubs . . . there'd be one black girl and 'fore we know it he'd have her cornered up. Wouldn't leave shit for me or Kahleel."

Tommy smiles politely and nods, but I can tell it bothers him. My sincere hope is this is because Shane was supposed to be in a relationship with Megan and not a racist reaction, but I don't know him well enough to be sure, and this deep in the Deep South you can never be sure.

Jayson shoots Rashard a look and he drops the subject.

A moment of awkward, uncomfortable silence passes.

"Shane was nice to everyone," Honor says. "Accepted everyone. And was liked by everyone."

"He really was," Kahleel adds.

"Good soldier," Josh says. "Good man. What else is there to be?"

Kayden, who has been particularly attentive to our table, coming back often to check on us, brings our food when she returns this time, rolling it out on a large old rusty red toolbox with casters on it.

As we eat and the boys share stories about Shane, I try to figure out a way to have a private conversation with Jayson. I want to find out if what's going on with him and Kayden has anything to do with Shane and to see if there's anything he doesn't feel like he can say in front of Tommy.

186

Chapter Thirty-six

"You flatter a girl," Jayson says.

I smile. "How so?"

"Working so hard to get me alone."

It has taken some maneuvering, but I finally managed it. I guess my efforts were just a little more transparent than I realized.

While the other boys take Tommy to Commando, the military supply store back up Victory Drive on the way to the base, I hang back ostensibly to make a couple of calls. At my suggestion, Jayson stays back with me so that he can show me how to get there and so Tommy can spend more time with Shane's friends.

It was weak but it worked, and it doesn't even matter if everyone thinks I was trying to get Jayson alone for other reasons.

"What can you tell me about Shane that you couldn't say in front of his brother? Oh, but before you get to that, what happened to Carl?"

He twists his lips up and raises his eyebrows. "Tragic accident. Beyond that . . . I don't know for sure. It's very rare that both your chutes don't work. Very rare. Most of the time . . . the guy panics, waits too late to pull the chute . . . or he jumps too late. First chute doesn't work and he freaks out and doesn't pull the second or . . . like I said . . . pulls it too late."

I nod. "Thanks. How about Shane? Anything you wouldn't say in front of his brother?"

He shrugs again. "Nothing, really. What we said about him was true. He was truly a good guy, treated everybody the same, worked hard—all the things we already said."

"Why didn't you want his brother to hear that he liked black girls?"

"I don't know exactly—except it looked like it made him uncomfortable and if it wasn't something Shane wanted him to know, it wasn't our place to tell him."

"What's the deal with Kayden?"

"Our waitress?"

"Yeah."

"Nothin'. Whatta you mean?"

"This is an official investigation into the suspicious death of someone I thought was a friend of yours."

"He is. I mean was. Why *suspicious?*"

"Tell me why she was here," I say. "Why she toasted him. Why she acted like we were her only table. Why she knows so much about Shane."

"They were seeing each other, all right? Damn. I didn't want to say anything because they were keepin' it on the DL."

Kayden lives in a mobile home park beneath Georgia pines and filled with chinaberry, black walnut, and cedar trees, down a side street behind Sweet Willy's. I drive back to the address Jayson gave me and park close to the old, faded-yellow single wide house trailer and get out.

As I'm approaching the place, Kayden comes out in an American flag bikini and white flip-flops, a white towel draped over her arm.

She stops when she sees me and starts shaking her head.

"I knew you were going to be a problem," she says. "The brother not so much, but you . . . you don't miss much, do you?"

"I miss plenty," I say.

She is pretty, but that's not what's most attractive about her. It's the figure revealed by the bikini that provides her true allure—the way her breasts and backside are perfectly proportioned. And the way there is plenty of each. It's also the color of her smooth skin, which reminds me of heavily creamed coffee.

"Mind if I ask you a few questions?" I say.

"Mind if we do it by the pool?" she says. "Don't have long before I have to be at my second job and I'm in need of a little pool time."

"Lead the way."

She leads me to the small cement pool in the center of the park and less than twenty feet from her home, passes through an opening in the tattered chain-link fence, tosses her towel on one of the rickety old plastic chaise lounge chairs, sits on the edge of the dirty and dilapidated old pool, and dangles her long caramel legs down in the murky water.

Clearly the pool hasn't been cleaned in—maybe ever. The leaves and branches and twigs of nearby overgrown trees have littered the pool until its waters are as tannic as those of the Dead Lakes.

"Are you sure that's safe?" I ask.

She smiles, looking up at me so that I see myself reflected in her shades.

Standing above her the way I am, I can see far too much of her breasts, which are barely covered by the bikini top.

Stepping over, I grab one of the plastic chairs, pull it up close to her, and sit on the end.

"I knew with the way Jayson was acting you were gonna pick up on . . . He loves to be in on secrets, but gives them away without ever saying a word."

Though the pool looks like a naturally occurring backwater bog, it still smells strongly of chemicals.

"Seriously," I say. "Are you sure it's safe to stick even your legs in there?"

"I'll shower off when I go in," she says. "But the pool is the reason I moved into this place and by God I'm gonna use it."

I nod.

"So they did the gathering at Sweet Willy's so you could be a part of it?" I ask.

"They did it there because it's Shane's favorite place, but yeah, also to let me feel less like a mistress I guess. I say *they*, but it was Jayson. He's the only one who really knows. The others may have seen us flirt or even hang out, but . . . Jayson's the only one who knew what it really was."

"Which was?"

"Love," she says, her expression and tone saying *duh*. "True love."

"How long were y'all together?" I ask.

"I'd rather not say, but a while. He tried and tried to break it off with Megan, but . . . she just wouldn't let him.

She's so . . . sad and sort of needy. He felt so bad for her. Hell, *I* felt bad for her, but . . ."

"He went home this past weekend to break up with her in person?" I say.

She nods. "Wouldn't let him do it any other way. Poor thing. He was dreading the mess out of it, but he felt so guilty he had to do it. She knew what was coming and didn't make it any easier on him. She certainly wasn't one for bowing out gracefully."

We are quiet a moment.

"I still can't believe he's gone," she says.

"How are you about it?" I ask. "You seem like you're doing okay."

"It's not real to me yet," she says. "I'm not sure it ever will be, but . . . it's certainly not now. It's just like he's still on his trip."

I nod. "When was the last time you spoke to him?"

"He was driving down to swim in the river," she says. "Said Megan was following him and he was going to tell her as soon as they got there."

Chapter Thirty-seven

"DADDY," Johanna squeals when I walk in the door.

She is sitting at the kitchen table looking at a book. Taylor is not far from her in a windup baby swing. Anna is standing at the stove cooking dinner.

"How are my girls?" I say.

"Better now," Anna says.

I kiss her and make my way over and kiss our daughters.

"Will you read this book to me, Daddy?"

"I'd love to," I say. "How about we do that right after supper?"

She nods her little head. "Okay, Daddy. That will be fine."

I smile.

I grab a Diet Cherry Coke from the fridge and step back over toward Anna. Coming up behind her, I press my body into hers as I hug her.

"How was your day?" I ask.

"It's been great. I love having her here. How'd it go?"

"Want me to help you finish up and then tell you

over dinner?"

"Perfect," she says.

So?" Anna says. "How was it?"

The four of us are sitting around the table well into working on our spaghetti. Johanna, who doesn't want any help, is twisting her noodles around her fork, getting more sauce on her face than in her mouth.

"Seemed very cathartic for Tommy," I say. "They all genuinely liked Shane. He really enjoyed being with them, hearing their stories, feeling a part of that part of Shane's life."

"I appreciate you going with him," she says. "I know you didn't have time, but . . . it really means a lot."

"Happy to."

"How was it for you?"

"Illuminating."

"Oh yeah? How so?"

"I met the girl Shane was breaking up with Megan for."

Her eyebrows shoot up. "Should've guessed it," she says. "People rarely ever break up with someone except to be with someone else. What's she like?"

"I liked her," I say. "She's smart, resourceful, attractive. I see what he saw in her."

She nods. "I feel so bad for Megan."

"Me too. And Tommy really does. She's in his youth group. He talked about her much of the way home. Her mom's a mess. He and Michelle have thought about taking her in. Always stopped short of doing it because of Shane. But now . . ."

"Might help them. Know it would her."

"Where does Tommy fall on the racism spectrum?" I ask.

She looks alarmed. "Why? What did he say?"

"Shane was hiding his new girlfriend from him and now she and his friends still are. I was wondering if it's because she's black or because he was seeing her while he was still supposed to be with Megan."

"Oh," she says, nodding as she thinks about it. "Interesting."

"She said Shane had broken up with Megan, but Megan refused to let him. Said he came home last weekend to do it in person."

"I'd've said Tommy's not racist at all," she says. "But I can't be sure of something like that—sometimes people really surprise you. Sometimes it's the ones you'd never suspect. I hope he's not like that. Hope he wasn't and that Shane didn't think he was."

Before I can express my agreement, my phone vibrates and I pull it out of my pocket.

It's Susan.

"Hey," I say. "How's it going? Getting settled in okay?"

"I don't think I can do this, John," she says. "I miss her too much."

They were the words I was most dreading to hear, the words some part of me expected to hear.

I frown and whisper to Anna, and excuse myself from the table to take the call.

Chapter Thirty-eight

"It's just an adjustment," I say. "It's difficult, but you can do it. After we talk, I'll put her on the phone and you can have a nice long visit."

"You don't understand," she says.

"Actually, I do," I say. "I know exactly what you're going through. It's something I go through all the time. Experiencing it like this will help you understand where I've been coming from, what I've been going through."

"I don't know," she says.

"You can do this," I say. "We both can. We can do it because it's what's right and good for her. We can make this work because we love her and want what is best for her. Because we care for each other and each want the other to have time with her too."

"I thought I could, but I don't think I can," she says. "I'm just so alone up here. I feel so lost without her."

"That's only because you're in the transition period. Once you have your full life up there again—a routine, friends, work . . . Why don't you call some of your old friends and go out?"

"I've tried. Everybody's busy. It's like they forgot about me, like they're not even glad I'm back."

"I'm sure that's not the case. Give it a little time.

You've only been up there a day. You'll reconnect with your old friends and make new ones. You should definitely do something tonight, though. Don't just sit around by yourself feeling lonely."

"I just don't think I can. I . . . I think if I go anywhere, it will be to get in my car and come get Johanna."

"Susan, listen to me," I say. "You can do this. We can. We've got to make this work. We've got an agreement in place. We have to stick to it, remember? You're just feeling overwhelmed. You're taking a big step. Take a breath. Think about the long-term. Don't let your momentary loneliness and fear defeat you. See this for the adventure it is and get on with it. Okay? Do something. Go shopping. I know you need things for your house. Go to a play or concert, a nice restaurant, club or bar. Go to an Al-Anon meeting. Keep calling your friends. Don't give up. Someone will say yes. Okay? Try. Please. You can do this."

She's gonna be a problem for the rest of our lives," Anna says.

While Johanna talks to Susan on the phone, Anna and I clean the kitchen and load the dishwasher.

"Maybe not," I say. "I was able to talk her down off the ledge tonight."

"So you're gonna do that every time she has a crisis?"

"It's gonna be okay," I say.

She twists her mouth up into a frown and gives me a look like she's not convinced.

"Dinner was delicious," I say. "Thank you again."

"The thing is . . ." she says. "You help people. That's

what you do. Hell, you just got back from spending the day in Columbus because Tommy asked you to—even though you had so much you needed to be doing here."

She pauses, but I don't say anything because I know she's not done.

"Sometimes you help people too much."

I start to ask if that's really even possible, but decide that's far too flippant, and instead think about what she's saying.

"You've got to have more boundaries," she says.

I nod to let her know I'm considering what she's saying.

"I want to be your first priority," she says. "I don't want you having to help your ex-wife all the time."

She drops a dish in the sink and it lands loudly.

"Shit," she says. "I don't want to be this person."

"What person?"

"Jealous. Petty. Needy."

"Hey," I say, taking her into my arms. "You're none of those things."

Our hands are wet and dampen our clothes where we touch.

"You're my first priority—you and the girls. If I ever do anything that makes you feel like you're not, you tell me immediately. Okay?"

"I'm being silly," she says. "I'm sorry."

"No you're not. This is my fault. I need—"

"I don't want to change you," she says. "I adore you. I love how you are, how quick you are to help anyone. Everyone."

"I know you're not trying to change me," I say. "But I need to change. I need more boundaries. I need to say no more. And I will. You'll help me."

"This isn't about that and you know it," she says. "This is about me being jealous. It's about me wanting to be the only woman you talk down off the ledge. This is about me dreading shit that's not going to happen. I just saw her as an ever-increasing part of our lives . . . and I freaked out a little."

"I promise you I'm not gonna let that happen," I say.

"I know."

"And you're right about the other too. I need better boundaries. Especially now. I'll need your help with it. Just know this—you are my priority, so if I ever do anything that makes you feel like you're not, tell me, because it's not intentional and I won't be aware of it."

We are still in our embrace when Johanna walks up with the phone.

"Mommy wants to speak to you," she says.

I hesitate but then reach for the phone.

"No," Johanna says. "Anna."

"Me?" she says, taking the phone.

It's a short conversation that ends with Anna saying, "You're very welcome."

"What was that?" I ask when she's off the call.

"Johanna told her what a good time we had today and how happy she was and Susan wanted to thank me for it."

Before she's even finished saying it my phone is buzzing again.

It's the prison. Looking at the display, I see I have several missed calls and messages.

Chapter Thirty-nine

"**I**f you can't get them to come out peacefully," the captain is saying, "then we're sending CERT in with chemical agents and weapons, and it won't be pretty."

We are standing outside the chapel. All around us members of the Correctional Emergency Response Team in full riot gear prepare to breach the building.

"It won't come to that," I say. "Just give me time. We can resolve this without anyone getting hurt."

Inside the chapel, a large group of inmates are staging a Black Lives Matter protest, refusing to come out and return to their dorms after being ordered to do so.

"Just give me time," I say again.

I open the door and walk into the chapel, down the main hallway past my office, through another door, and into the sanctuary.

There are far more men than I expect.

They are on the floor and on the pews, their arms locked together in the classic sit-in fashion.

As I make my way along the back and then down the center aisle, they have to unlink arms to let me through.

Passing through them, I pray for inspired words to share and a peaceful resolution to this situation.

When I reach the front, I step onto the platform and

look out at the sea of black faces and the few white ones mixed in.

From in the crowd, someone yells, "BLACK LIVES MATTER."

I shake my head. "No," I say. "They never have the way they should in this country."

The chapel goes as silent as I've ever heard it with a congregation in it.

"That's why we have this movement," I say. "That's why so many people are standing up or sitting in and saying something that should be true but isn't—not the way it should be, not in this great country that gets so many things right. Black lives matter. Black lives should matter more than they do."

Some of the men nod, most just continue to stare.

"Do you know whose lives really matter most in our culture?" I say.

"YOURS," someone yells.

"WHITE LIVES," someone else says.

"SHUT UP AND LET THE MAN SPEAK," someone shouts.

"Wealthy lives," I say. "Powerful lives. Celebrity lives. Those are the lives we seem to value. And yes, they are largely though not exclusively white lives. It's not right. It's not okay. Which is why we have to change it. That's what this movement is about. It's about saying all lives should matter equally and they don't. It's about speaking truth to power and saying it's not okay to shoot unarmed citizens in the streets. It's not okay to incarcerate masses of young black men. Injustice is not okay. Inequality is not okay. Institutional and social systems of oppression that keep large segments of our populations in the prison of generational poverty are not okay. So we speak out. So we stand up. So we sit in."

"SO WHY DO WE HAVE TO LEAVE?" someone yells.

"YEAH."

"To have the moral authority to speak out against immorality, we must be the most moral, must set a standard for ourselves and carry ourselves with such humility and dignity and righteousness that we lend credence and credibility to our cause. If, as Dr. King said, 'Injustice anywhere is a threat to justice everywhere,' then we must not act unjustly in our attempt to bring about justice. Recall what Dr. King said. 'Darkness cannot drive out darkness. Only light can do that. Hate cannot drive out hate. Only love can do that.' Remember the words of Jesus, too. 'Love your enemies. Bless those who curse you. Pray for those who persecute you.'"

"SO DO NOTHING?"

"That's not what I'm saying. You've already done something. You've gathered. You've borne witness. You've made a stand. I'm saying don't undo the good you've done by turning this into something it shouldn't be, into something that could get somebody hurt. Realize this. You are in prison. You are limited in what you can do. The best use of your time is to get yourself right, ready, educated, healed, together, so that when you go back out into the world, you can be a part of the solution and not part of the problem. These are very complex problems and will take the majority of us working together to solve. They have more to do with poverty and fear and frustration and desperation than race and weapons. We are all responsible. Here's what I propose . . ."

I pause a moment to make sure they are all listening.

"Return to your dorms peacefully. Don't antagonize or escalate. Be courteous and respectful. Conduct yourselves with the honor and dignity that this cause deserves. And we'll host a series of Black Lives Matter programs and events here at the chapel beginning this weekend. We'll have guest speakers and music—positive programs that will remind everyone that Black Lives Matter, that will make this prison in particular and the world in general a better place. Will you do that? Will you line up and follow me out? Will you leave peacefully with me now knowing that something good has been started today?"

"That was good work in there tonight, Chaplain," the captain is saying.

We are walking toward the main gate in the soft glow of low evening sunlight.

He shakes his head. "Black lives matter, what about cops' lives? White lives? CO lives?"

I stop walking.

He stops too.

"Yeah, saying 'black lives matter' means 'cop lives don't matter,'" I say, "in the same way that when Jesus said 'blessed are the poor' he didn't want anyone else to be blessed, or to say 'save the whales' means 'kill the dolphins.'"

"I don't get it," he says.

"For a group of people who have been oppressed and abused and enslaved and treated worse than any group in this country—except the native people—to assert that their lives matter when they see kids and unarmed men be-

202

ing killed in the streets doesn't in anyway take away from all lives mattering. It's like the people who complain about us having a Black History Month. 'Why don't we have a white history month?' they say. Because every month is white history month. Because all the Eurocentric history textbooks leave out so much. Because we're reclaiming something that has been missed, omitted, left out, undervalued. And when that is done, when someone asks or even demands equality, it doesn't diminish yours. One group having rights doesn't take away from the rights of another group—unless, of course, one group's so-called rights are actually privileges predicated on the oppression of other groups."

"Well, I just don't see it that way," he says. "And I'm gonna recommend to the warden that he not approve any Black Lives Matter rallies. And I've got the majority of the officers behind me, so . . . prepare yourself for a fight."

Later that night, Johanna and I have a tea party in her bedroom.

Her room is small and it has Taylor's crib in it, and though there are larger bedrooms upstairs, we're not comfortable with either of our daughters not being on the same floor with us until they're older.

I'm sitting at a tiny table in a tiny chair, my knees around my ears, across from a stylish teddy bear named Huggie. Johanna sits next to us, a doll with big brown eyes meant to resemble her in the chair opposite her.

Johanna is busy pouring the tea from her tiny china teapot into our tiny teacups, talking nonstop as she does.

As I sit here listening to the workings of her little mind while watching the workings of her little hands, Huggie staring at me blankly with his big button eyes, his fedora tilted down a bit on his head, I feel what I so often feel these days—a joy so profound it seems spiritual, so deep it seems bottomless.

The peace and love and happiness Anna and I have achieved together seems earned in a way—though it only partly is—but the ecstatic happiness I experience with Johanna seems an altogether unexpected gift and still catches me by surprise.

Chapter Forty

Early the next morning, Sam, Reggie, and I meet to discuss the case, get an update on forensics, and for them to tell me about what I missed while I was in Columbus.

We are meeting early as an accommodation for me because I'll be at my job at the prison all day.

"How was your trip?" Reggie asks.

"Good. Thanks for letting me go. And it actually resulted in some more info for us, though I don't think it has any bearing on what happened."

They both look interested, indicating for me to tell them more.

"Shane had a girlfriend up there—which is why he was breaking up with Megan. An older, more mature girlfriend. Name is Kayden, and she said Shane tried to break up with Megan many times and Megan wouldn't let him. Said she knew what was coming."

"That's good to know," Reggie says. "Until yesterday I liked her best for doing something—if something was done."

"Did you release a statement and send a counselor over to see her?" I ask.

"I did, but the paper doesn't come out until tomorrow, so word hasn't really gotten out yet."

"What about a counselor?"

"I made the referral but don't know if she's seen her yet. But why coddle her if she could have killed Shane?"

"Because we don't even know he was killed," I say. "But even if he was . . . that's not how we seek justice—to let her be smeared and vilified on Facebook and Twitter and in town talk. It's brutal. And it's out of hand."

"It's funny . . ." Sam says. "I never really realized it until now, but . . . John is the girl of this investigation."

"Call me whatever you want, just do right by that young girl."

Reggie looks at Sam and says, "Wonder if he'll feel differently once he hears about the bowline?"

"From her Jet Ski?" I say. "What about it?"

"It's missing," she says. "She swears it was on there when she put in at Iola. Got a witness who says so too."

"But under that theory, if Vera is right and Shane was snatched under, then it was most likely an accident. His foot got tangled up in the rope, it snatched him under when she took off, he got caught on something under the water, and she never knew it even happened."

"She could've done it on purpose," Sam says.

"Sure, but that's far less likely, and whether she did it on purpose, it was an accident, or she had absolutely nothing to do with it, the way we treat her should be the same—humane, compassionate, fair, impartial, and not allow the media, social or otherwise, to skewer a kid for murder when we don't even know if there was a murder yet."

Reggie nods. "Okay. I don't see it quite that way, but I respect what you're saying and will follow up on it."

"It's preliminary," Sam says, "but our lab techs say they believe there was human blood on the blade of the knife used to carve the crucifix in the tree at Iola Landing and it's possible that at least one but probably more of Amber's wounds were made with a knife like the one used on the tree. Since the carving was made before she was taken, the blood on the tree could be the killer's or a previous victim's. Either way it's good evidence that can help us with identities and or apprehension—or at least in building a case for trial."

I nod. "That's good."

"Real good," Reggie says.

"Has the lab identified what the cross was made of?" I ask.

Sam shakes her head.

"I keep thinking I should be able to," I say. "I need to take another look at it."

"You want to see the actual cross or will pictures do?" Sam says.

"Can start with pictures and see," I say.

"I'll get them and we can look at them together."

"Thanks," I say.

"Oh," Reggie says, "almost forgot. Amber's phone was finally turned back on for a few minutes yesterday, but then it was turned right back off again. Verizon pinged it, but by the time deputies arrived at the location, the phone and guy with it was gone."

"Where was it?"

"Outside of Orlando."

"So what else did I miss yesterday? Why did you say Megan was your leading suspect up until then?"

She smiles. "Because we caught Matt and Cody sneaking into the landing last night to get the big-ass stash they had hidden when Shane disappeared and we were called."

"Where was it?"

"In weighted down garbage bags underwater. They had put it over in the little slough on the park side of the boat launch."

"Bags?" I say. "As in more than one?"

"Three. All full. All filled with some truly nasty shit. We're talking amounts large enough to send them away for a long time. And more than large enough to kill for. We're thinking maybe Shane was killed by them or some of their associates. He's a ra-ra Ranger. Captain Do the Right Thing. Maybe he threatened to turn them in. Maybe they just assumed he would and didn't want to take any chances."

"They both told me Shane not only drank but did drugs with them," I say. "Given his chosen career and how well he was doing in it, I find it hard to believe he did. They could've said it in an attempt to explain what happened to him—or because they knew we would find it in his system from where they slipped it to him and were already laying the groundwork for accidental drowning, contributed to by alcohol and drugs use. I wish I knew who suggested the race across the river. They could've slipped him something and challenged him to the race to get him to drown. And maybe that's exactly what happened, only it was a little delayed because of all his training and the great shape he was in. I wish we knew what was in his system."

"We would if we had found the body," Reggie says. "Can't believe we haven't."

"Would help everything," I say. "What he was on. Whether we're even dealing with a murder or not."

"I only have one more thing," Reggie says. "Saved the most outlandish for last. Tommy said he saw footprints on the path over on the opposite bank behind the house-boat."

"Yeah, I saw them," I say.

"He started talking about Shane not being dead, about him getting dazed and wandering out over there or, even crazier, said it could be where his killers came in to kill him. Even speculated it was military related—like ISIS or some shit like that. Out there. But . . . we sent a deputy over with a search and rescue guy and guess what—the houseboat had been broken into. Something that happens all the time on the river. Usually kids, breaking in to screw or drink or smoke, so I didn't take it very seriously, but now . . . I've at least got to ask . . . What if that's where the drug deal went down? Or maybe where it was supposed to. What if Matt and Cody's suppliers were over there? What if Shane saw them or saw something he wasn't supposed to when they swam over there? What if that's what got him killed?"

Chapter Forty-one

"So when did you become a drug dealer?" I ask Cody.

Unable to help myself, I had called the warden and told him I'd be in a little late so I could interview Matt and Cody before I left St. Joe.

No matter what I tried, Matt refused to say a single word to me, so I am now working on Cody.

"It was smart to put the small stash in the bathroom for us to find," I say. "We thought that's all there was. Whose idea was that? Thought y'all were just doing some drugs. Had no idea y'all were big time drug dealers."

"Man, I ain't no drug dealer," he says. "Don't even play like that."

"I'm not playing. I really want to know."

"I don't deal drugs. Never have. Never will."

"You could be in college right now," I say. "Playing baseball. Having new experiences. Learning new ways to think. Meeting girls. Why deal poison to people instead of doing that?"

"I don't deal poison to people," he says. "I already told you. I also already told you that I plan to go back to college in the fall. Tryin' out for several teams."

"Off the record," I say. "I really am just trying to

understand. You see, I try to help people when I can. I work with a lot of addicts and inmates and young people, and I'm really trying to understand how someone with your opportunities and advantages does something like this. Honestly. I'm genuinely curious."

He studies me for a long moment, seeming to assess the veracity of what I'm saying.

"Off the record?" he asks.

I nod, as if there is any such thing.

"Let's say what I do . . . what I allegedly do—you know, just pretend make believe so I can play along with your game and try to answer your hypothetical questions— is in wholesale not retail. Let's say what I do is favors for friends—like say picking up something or dropping off something, like a couch or something. And sometimes may- be I help them out with storage, you know? Like I hold on to the couch for them for a little while. Never long. No big deal. None of it is a big deal at all. And for these favors my friends throw a little cash my way. That's it. Nothing to it."

"Why?" I say. "That's what I'm asking. Why do any of these favors for these friends at all?"

He shrugs. "Do what you can for your friends. And the same reason everybody does what they do—man's got to eat, got to pay his bills."

"Did it start before you went off to college? Did you do it there? Or—"

"Just since I've been back," he says. "Since I got cut from the team and hurt my knee and had to readjust my whole entire fuckin' life 'cause shit doesn't work out like you think it's going to."

"Did Shane know about it?"

"Shane was cool," he says.

"Is that a *yes?*"

He nods.

"He ever do any favors for friends?"

"No."

"Or just help you? You're his friend."

"No. Never. Couldn't mess around with shit like that. He get caught . . . and his promising career would be over. His uncle wasn't understanding at all."

"His uncle?"

"Uncle Sam," he says with a self-satisfied smile, as if he had said something clever. "Had too much to lose."

"If that's the case, then why was he drinking the way he was and doing the Xanbars with y'all?"

"I wondered that too," he says. "I really did. It wasn't like him. Hell, it was the first time he ever did something like that."

Chapter Forty-two

After work, I drive to the landing to check in.

My day at the prison had been difficult and draining—counseling, teaching, crisis intervention, and arguing with the warden about the need for a series of Black Lives Matter programs in the chapel. It had taken some convincing, but I finally persuaded him when I explained the programs wouldn't be all that different from the Black History Month programs we do every February and that doing them would have a huge impact on inmate morale and the security of the institution.

I am tired and sleepy and all I want to do is be with Anna and the girls, but I feel like I need to check in with Ralph and the search and rescue workers and volunteers since I hadn't been able to at all the previous day.

There are far fewer workers and volunteers this evening. The ones who are still around appear to be living here. Camping. Cooking. Socializing.

"Still nothing," Ralph says as I walk up. "But we're just getting started and we're not going anywhere."

I nod, looking around the landing.

"How's everyone holding up?" I ask.

"Good," he says. "We're used to this. We set up

camp and make it as pleasant as possible for everyone as we can."

"Seems like far fewer people around," I say.

He nods. "Attrition. Always happens. But it's good for us. Our core group gets a lot more done when it's just us. Helps when the family's not around too. We don't have to do so much for show and we don't have to worry about something they might see upsetting them."

"Tommy here?"

"Was earlier. Left just a little while ago. Meeting with someone from the army about Shane's affairs, then had something at the church I think. Said he'd be back but I think it'll be awhile. Maybe even tomorrow."

"Doesn't matter. I was just going to check on him while I was here."

"Gotcha."

"Have you found anything out of the ordinary?" I ask.

"Whatta you mean?"

"Anything that shouldn't be down there," I say. "I don't mean a sunken boat or old rusted car part, but anything recent that doesn't make sense or you can't explain?"

"No, not really," he says. "But we'll let you know if we do."

I'm driving away from the landing when Sam calls.

"Where are you?" she asks.

I tell her.

"Got the pictures of the cross for you," she says. "Buy me a drink and I'll show you 'em."

"Pick a place," I say. "You've got two options. Tucks

only has beer and wine, but they have good food. Twenty-two has a full bar."

"Wewa is a two-bar town?" she asks. "Don't think I've heard of either one of those places."

"Tucks is actually Tukedawayz Tavern and Twenty-two is the old Highway 22 Package and Lounge out on Highway 22. I'll see if we can find a sitter and get Anna to join us."

"Then let's do Tucks and eat too."

Which is how the three of us are at a table at Tucks thirty minutes later.

It took half an hour to get here because I went by our house to see the girls and pick Anna up.

In the dim bar, from a distance I wonder if people looking in our direction believe Anna and I have a child with us.

This calls to mind the line that Reggie sometimes quotes from *Sweet Home Alabama*. "You have a *baby*—in a *bar*."

"So Johanna, the perfect combination of your two names, is not your daughter?" Sam is saying.

"She's ours," Anna says. "They both are ours, but no, I didn't give birth to her and her mother certainly didn't intend to combine our names. She chose it as a namesake for John, but I think it's . . . kinda magic that it's our names joined."

"Yes, it is," I say without looking up.

I'm looking at lab photos of the cross while the ladies drink beer and talk.

"What is that?" I say. "I feel like I should know."

"Let's see," Anna says.

I glance at Sam. "I can show her now in front of you

or later at home behind your back," I say.

She smiles and nods. And I hand a couple of the photos to Anna.

It's early and there are very few people in Tucks—a handful around the bar, for or five around the two pool tables, and the three of us at one of the three small tables near the door.

Like all the other places where people gather in town, the two most prevalent topics of conversation are Shane being missing and the crucified girl they pulled out of the water.

The jukebox continues to play classic country songs because a huge white man in a wife beater and straw cowboy hat fed a twenty into the machine and stood there for fifteen minutes making his selections. At the moment it's Patsy Cline's "Walkin' After Midnight."

The FDLE lab photos are labeled and numbered and show the cross in a variety of positions—first with Amber's body still attached, then after it had been removed, then each section from several angles including extreme close-ups.

The lengths of metal are about four inches in diameter and four feet long. Hollow and rectangular, they have traces of white paint and rust on them. Two of them have a few small holes but only on one side.

"They do look familiar," Anna says, "but . . ."

"We won't know just how significant they are to the killer until we find another victim and see if he used them on her," Sam says.

"He did," I say. "Everything he did and used and took is significant to him."

She nods. "Daniel says the same thing."

"And he would know," I say.

"Wonder how many other crucified victims there are out there waiting to be found?" Sam says.

"Wonder if they're all in bodies of water?" Anna says.

"My guess is they are," I say. "He's combining crucifixion and baptism, death and rebirth."

"Walkin' After Midnight" ends and Tammy Wynette's "Stand by Your Man" comes on.

"Wonder how big a radius he's using?" she says. "And if he's dumping them only in the Apalachicola River or only in rivers, or in lakes and bays too?"

"Great questions," Sam says. "Wish we had more to go on. Guess we will soon enough."

Peach, one of the owners, brings our food over and catches sight of the photos. "Oh hell, John," she says, shuddering all over and covering her eyes.

She is small and short and wears jeans, a camo three-quarter sleeve T-shirt with a hunting logo on it, and round-toed cowgirl boots like Reggie. Unlike Reggie, she has a snuff can in her back pocket and a dip inside her bottom lip.

"Sorry."

"You tryin' to scar me for life or run off my customers?" she says. "Nah, I'm just kiddin'. Do what y'all got to do to find that bastard and string him up by his balls. Or call me and I'll help you take him in the swamp and feed him to some gators."

As Peach walks away, Sam says, "That's a call you'd never make, is it?"

"What's that?"

"Trying to find your own justice."

"What makes you think I haven't before?" I say.

"The way you are about the Stripling girl," she says. "She could be a killer but you want her treated with— what?"

"Civility. Humanity. Compassion. And maybe the reason I am the way I am is because I *have* made that call before."

She shakes her head and smiles. "Nope. No way. Good try there, Slim, but I don't buy it."

"The bullying's gettin' worse," Anna says. "I can't get over what people—her classmates and their parents—post on Facebook."

"Social media's a little window right into people's hearts and minds and black souls. It's like suspects. Let them talk long enough and they'll reveal exactly who they are."

"Well, who we are is sad and sick and scary," Anna says.

"Some more than others," Sam says, as we put the pictures away and begin to pull open the food containers. "Some more than others."

The food is hot and spicy and so good I wish we had ordered more, but we don't even get to finish it.

We're less than halfway through our meal when the first call comes in.

Chapter Forty-three

"Shit never comes in when you're in the middle of something you don't want to be doing," Sam says as she stands and steps away to take the call.

While she's away my phone vibrates.

A few minutes later, when she returns to the table, Sam says, "We've got another body."

"Actually," I say, holding up my phone, "we have two."

"Now that we know for sure we're dealing with a serial," Sam says, "I'd like us to talk about exactly what that means and how we approach this case."

Two more victims with striking similarities to Amber had been discovered—one in the Apalachicola Bay, the other in Tampa Bay.

Sam, Reggie, and I are driving to the scene in Apalachicola.

I'm driving. Sam is in the passenger seat. Reggie is in the back.

"Now that we have at least two other victims spread

way out," Reggie says, "it's really, really doubtful that whatever happened to Shane is related to what happened to
Amber, right?"

"I'd say so," Sam says, then looks over at me.

I nod. "Don't think we can rule it out until we can,
but, yes, very, very doubtful."

"I've had Daniel working on a profile," she says,
"but he was uncomfortable doing it when by definition we
didn't have a serial killer yet."

"By definition," Reggie says. "What is the definition? I don't have any experience in this area."

"Not many people do," I say. "Only about one
percent of all murders is committed by a compulsive killer.
But what about the case you worked last year with the cops
being killed with their own guns?"

"That was different," she says dismissively. "Nothing
at all like this. I wonder how much I know or think I do is
wrong? Most of it has come from documentaries and mov-
ies."

Sam says, "A serial killer is someone, usually a white
male acting alone, who murders three or more people—
usually with what seems like no motive, but is actually
an internal motive, the gratification of a deep abnormal
psychological obsession—over more than a month with a
significant break or cooling off period between them."

"They often appear to lead very normal lives," I say.
"Wear a mask of sanity, but usually do menial work, man-
ual labor—something they're overqualified for. Everything
comes down to fantasy for them—everything. Their fantasies are what motivate them, what cause them to do what
they do, the reason they take trophies—so they can relive
the event and fantasize about it over and over. They can

be in a relationship, but like their job it's a source of frustration for them. They usually abuse alcohol and or drugs, have money problems. They're usually of average intelligence. Usually average in most every way."

Sam says, "They almost always have unresolved, fucked-up issues with their mothers."

"Suffer psychological, sexual, and physical trauma in childhood—usually from a family member," I say.

"Often have head injuries because of it," Sam adds. "Repeated head injuries are common."

"Their childhoods and adolescences were spent in isolation."

"Their fantasy lives start then," Sam says. "One theory is that as children they are powerless against the torment they are suffering, so the only way to escape is into fantasy. They can control everything in the self-centered world of fantasy and in there they are the only ones who matter. There's no empathy, no compassion, no mercy, no remorse. Eventually the worlds of their fantasies begins to spill over into their waking worlds. They wet the bed way past the age they should. They set fires. Act out their fantasies on animals. Their voyeurism usually begins back then too."

"As do certain fetishes and paraphilia," I say.

"Paraphilia?" Reggie asks.

Sam says, "Sexual arousal to shit that shouldn't sexually arouse you."

"Dangerous sexual deviance," I say. "Being sexually aroused by atypical objects and fantasies and fetishes and situations."

"Both of you have worked serial cases before?" Reggie asks.

Sam nods. "A few."

They both look at me.

I nod. "Couple of cases in Atlanta," I say. "The Atlanta Child Murders are what put me on this path in the first place. I worked it and a few cases connected to it and the Stone Cold Killer case. As a kid I watched as my dad worked the Bundy case. And I've also worked *with* several incarcerated serial murderers inside as a prison chaplain."

"So we have some experience on our team," Reggie says.

"Our *team* . . . is about to get a whole lot bigger," Sam says. "With a body as far down as Tampa Bay and us now having three . . . they'll form a multiagency task force and most likely the FBI will get involved. We solve it fast or we don't solve it at all."

"Then let's solve it fast," Reggie says.

"With a body as far away as Tampa Bay, the killer moves around," I say, "and is most likely long gone from our little town."

"Which is a good thing," she says, "but I sure would like for us to be the ones to take him off the board."

Apalachicola is a small former fishing town that is now a tourist destination, and is where the Apalachicola River flows into the bay—a freshwater flow that forms one of the most diverse estuaries and best oysters in the world.

The crucified victim was discovered when she became entangled in the giant nets of a shrimp boat.

It's dark by the time we arrive, and the dock, shrimp boat, body, and the edge of the river are all lit by huge banks of halogen lights.

The boat is moored at a dock in downtown, the area

taped off and surrounded by emergency vehicles, their flashing red and blue lights causing the locale to look more like a rave than a crime scene.

Within moments of being there we have the information we came for—confirmation it's the same killer.

The manner and method of death, the materials used, the victim herself—all so incredibly similar they could be the same.

"She could be Amber's sister," Sam says.

I nod.

"Means he's got a very definite type. Should help us figure out how and where he's finding them."

"Everything about her and what's he's done to her will lead us directly to him," I say. "We just have to figure out how."

Chapter Forty-four

I climb into bed beside Anna bone-weary and brain-dead.

She stirs and I pull her to me, wrapping her up in my arms and spooning her.

"There's nothing that can happen in a day so bad that this can't remedy," I say. "You are my sanctuary."

"You are mine," she says.

"How were the girls when you got back? How was the rest of the evening?"

"All good with the exception of one important thing," she says. "You weren't here."

I hug her even more tightly.

"Susan called," she says. "Wasn't happy you weren't here."

"What happened?"

"I handled it," she says. "You're not the only one who can talk a bitch down off a ledge."

I laugh, squeeze her, then we lie in silence for a few moments.

Evidently I drift off, because she is saying something when I wake back up.

"Huh?" I say.

"Sorry. I didn't realize you had fallen asleep. We'll

talk in the morning."

"No. What? I didn't mean to fall asleep yet."

"I was just saying all small towns are alike when it comes to gossip," she says. "It's unbelievable how quickly rumors run through a place like this."

"Even faster now because of cell phones and Facebook," I say.

"Don't even get me started on Facebook," she says.

"What's the town talk today?"

"A lot of it is still about Megan. That she killed him. That's she's pregnant and crazy with hormones and being scorned. That the baby is really Cody's and they did it together to protect their drug empire. That she's in a polyamorous relationship with Matt and Cody and they all run a drug empire together like the Oliver Stone movie that came out a few years back. Some people are saying that Shane's death is related to what he did for the military, that he was taken out in some sort of covert operation. But the one that's most hurtful to Tommy and Michelle is that he faked his own drowning and death because he's a coward who wanted out of the military."

"What's wrong with people?" I say.

"That's your department," she says. "I just live here."

"We need to check on Tommy and Michelle tomorrow," I say. "Megan too."

In another bed a few miles away, another couple is holding and talking.

Reggie says, "Are you awake?"

"Yeah," Merrick says. "Why? Did I jump?"

"John Jordan asked me about the cop killings today,"

she says.

"What'd you say?"

"Not much, but he could tell I was uncomfortable talking about it. I didn't handle it well at all. Thing is . . . it's not the first time he's asked me about it."

"You think he suspects something?" Merrick asks.

"I think he's a dangerous man to have around," she says. "And eventually he's gonna ask to take a look at the case, reopen it."

"I think you're overreacting," he says. "Worrying about something that will never happen. Hell, I think he'd understand, but . . . if you're that concerned . . . you could fire him before he gets a chance to."

Chapter Forty-five

"John," Anna says. "John, wake up. You've got to see this."

I rouse from a very deep sleep.

I have no idea what time it is, but sunlight streams in the edges around the blinds on our windows.

"Huh? What is it?"

She's holding her iPad in front of me.

"Look."

I blink and try to focus on what she's showing me.

With real effort I push myself up off the pillow and take the device from her.

The Facebook app fills the screen. A live video is streaming in the center of her newsfeed.

"What is it?"

"Not what. Who. It's Megan."

"What's she—"

She's in a small boat on the river. The camera is close to her distraught face and she's saying something.

"She says she's going to kill herself in front of everyone," Anna says.

"What?"

Dropping the device so I can still see it, I jump out of bed and back into my clothes still on the floor from the night before, watching the screen as I do.

"You guessed it," Megan is saying. "I'm not coming to school today. Not coming any day ever again. Happy now? Relieved to know the crazy ex-girlfriend killer won't be back."

"Can I take this?" I ask Anna, as I grab the device and dash out of the room.

Anna, who is moving with me through the house, nods. "Of course."

"Can you call Reggie and tell her what's going on? Can you look at it on your phone? See if y'all can find out where she is. Let search and rescue know. They're still on the river. Maybe someone can . . . See if we can call or text her. Thank you. Love you."

I am out the door, down the walkway, in my car, speeding toward the river.

As soon as the link between my phone and car is established, I give the voice command for it to call Tommy.

"John? Have they found him?"

"Sorry, man. I know you're in no shape to be . . . but she's in your youth group and you're Shane's brother. If anyone can get through to her."

"What is it? What's wrong?"

I tell him.

"I'm bringing it up now," he says. "Oh my God. I'm . . . I'm up. Gonna try to call her now. I'm heading to the landing. Call you back in a—"

The line goes dead, and I return my attention back to Anna's iPad.

People are beginning to comment beneath the video—kids, Megan's classmates, begging her not to do it. Apologizing to her for what's she's been through. Others are posting hugs and hearts and sad faces. Others, people I can't fathom are anything but psychopaths, are daring her to do it, telling her to quit being so dramatic, asking her if the guilt is finally getting to her.

". . . can take someone's life and just treat it like some reality show," Megan is saying. "You can't—I mean you can. You did. But you don't know me. You don't know what I'm capable of and what I'm not. You just make shit up about someone—a real human being who's devastated because her boyfriend, the best thing that's ever happened to her, is dead—just say whatever the fuck you want to, just trash a person you clearly don't know. You think I'm a killer? Well, I am—or I'm about to be. I didn't kill Shane. I could never . . . I loved him with all of my . . . Never kill him. But you want a killer. And I don't want to live in a world without Shane in it and where people like y'all want blood no matter whose it is."

My phone rings.

"Oh God, John," Reggie says. "I can't believe this is . . . We can't get through to her. Can't get her to pick up or respond. Where are you?"

"On Lake Grove Road," I say. "Just drove over the bridge. Where is she?"

"We think near Iola Landing. I'm on my way over to the Gaskin Park now to check. Can you go straight to Iola?"

"Yeah."

"If she's not there, I'll get one of the search and rescue boats to run upriver to see if we can find her. I don't know what else to do."

"Don't know there's anything else we can do," I say. "I'm turning onto the Iola road now."

We disconnect and I look at Anna's iPad again.

The video is gone.

Facebook has halted the live stream, taken the video down.

My phone vibrates.

"They stopped the video," Anna says. "Where are you? Everyone seems to think she's close to Iola."

"That's where I'm headed."

My phone vibrates again. I have another call coming in. It's Tommy.

"Tommy's calling," I say.

"Take it. Call me later. When you can. Love you."

"Love you."

I tap over to take his call.

"I've lost her, John," he says. "And she won't answer. I can't get her to pick up."

"Keep trying and come to Iola."

"Okay, but—"

"She's here," I say. "Gotta go."

I stomp on the brakes, throw the car into Park, and jump out.

"MEGAN," I yell, running down the boat launch to the water's edge.

The early morning is bright and quiet and comparatively cool, dew still clinging to hanging leaves and blades of grass.

She is standing in a small green boat out in the water, maybe fifty yards from the shore.

She has a revolver pointed just beneath her chin now and is still holding up her phone and talking into it.

"MEGAN, PLEASE DON'T DO THIS," I yell. "NOT BECAUSE OF A FEW IGNORANT BULLIES.

PLEASE. DON'T GIVE THEM THIS KIND OF POW-
ER OVER YOU. DON'T LET THEM HAVE THE LAST
WORD."

"I GET THE LAST WORDS," she yells back.
"THE VERY LAST. I DIDN'T KILL HIM. I DON'T
WANT TO LIVE WITHOUT HIM. I DON'T WANT
TO LIVE IN A WORLD WHERE PEOPLE ARE SO . . .
CRUEL AND HATEFUL."

Behind me Tommy screeches to a stop and jumps
out of his car.

"MEGAN," he yells. "PLEASE MEGAN. DON'T
DO THIS. I KNOW YOU DIDN'T HURT SHANE.
PLEASE STAY WITH US. SOON EVERYONE WILL
KNOW. HANG AROUND AND MAKE THEM APOL-
OGIZE TO YOU."

"TOMMY?"

"YEAH."

"TOMMY, SHANE AND I BOTH LOVED YOU.
YOU WERE LIKE A DAD TO BOTH OF US."

"I LOVE YOU, MEGAN. PLEASE DON'T
DO THIS. PLEASE. I'VE ALREADY LOST SHANE,
PLEASE DON'T MAKE ME LOSE YOU TOO. I
CAN'T TAKE ANY MORE LOSS. PLEASE, MEGAN."

"I'M SORRY. I LOVE YOU. AND I DIDN'T KILL
SHANE. I DIDN'T HAVE ANYTHING TO DO WITH
ANY DRUGS. I LOVED SHANE. THAT'S ALL."

"MEGAN. I COULD REALLY USE YOUR HELP
WITH SHANE'S MEMORIAL SERVICE. PLEASE
HELP ME WITH THAT. WOULD YOU? PLEASE. I'M
SO LOST WITHOUT HIM. I NEED ALL THE SUP-
PORT I CAN GET."

Coming upstream, easing toward Megan, still quite a

ways away, Reggie on a search and rescue boat can be seen in the distance.

"I'M NOT DOING THIS FOR ATTENTION. I'M NOT TRYING TO TAKE ANYTHING AWAY FROM SHANE'S . . . DEATH. I . . . I JUST CAN'T LIVE LIKE THIS, CAN'T . . . KEEP BEING CALLED A MON-STER. I'M SORRY. I REALLY AM, BUT . . ."

The shot shatters the silence of the early morning and echoes up and down the river and out into the swamps.

"NOOOO," Tommy and I yell, but she doesn't hear. She can't.

Her body pitches forward and falls into the water, sending ripples out on the surface that was smooth and still a second before. She vanishes into the river that has taken so very many and doesn't return, and I wonder if she or Shane ever will.

Chapter Forty-six

Shock.

Disbelief.

Sadness.

Most of the town is in mourning.

Most, but not all. Some, the same ones who contributed to Megan's death, the militantly malignant and pathologically self-important who refuse to let anything, including the death of a vulnerable teenage girl, alter their perspectives, change their minds, stir the least bit of compassion, continue to post ignorant and insensitive innuendo, questions, rants, and conspiracy theories.

Decent people mourn and most people are decent.

Like Shane's, Megan's body has not yet been recovered, so now search and rescue is searching for not one but two teens in our river for whom it's far too late for rescue.

"You were right," Reggie says to me. "I didn't realize just how distraught that little girl really was."

It is later in the evening of that same day and we are standing near search and rescue's mobile headquarters in the late-afternoon sun.

I shake my head. "I should've done more. Should've . . ."

"You're the only one who did anything."

"Didn't do enough. Not nearly enough."

Search and rescue now has two teams working two different areas of the river—upstream where Megan went into the water and downstream where Shane vanished.

Reggie looks out at the boats dragging the river for Shane's body.

"What if we never find him?" she says. "What if he's like Ralph's brother?"

It's a real possibility, one that seems to be increasing with every second that passes. I take her questions as rhetorical and don't answer. Even if they aren't rhetorical I don't have any answers.

We both turn as a car racing toward the landing ignores the deputy's orders to slow down and stop, crashes through the police barricade, and fishtails as it come to a smoking, screeching stop not far from us.

Megan's mother jumps out and runs toward us.

"Y'all let this happen," she says. "Y'all let everyone think she killed Shane. Y'all are the real killers. Killed my baby girl!"

Flailing about, she comes at us punching and kicking.

The deputy posted by the barricade is running up behind her.

I wrap my arms around her, holding her in a hug that keeps her from hitting us or hurting herself, though she continues to kick my lower legs.

"I'm sorry," I say. "I'm so sorry."

"Get your fuckin' hands off of me, you fuck. You

murderin' fuck."

I release her slowly and she punches me in the face.

The deputy coming up behind her grabs her and pulls her back.

"Help her get home," Reggie says. "I'll watch the entrance until you get back."

He starts to pull her back toward her car, but she collapses, dropping to the pavement and sobbing uncontrollably.

Later, long after Megan's mom has gone and the barricade has been repaired, Tommy pulls up to the landing and gets out.

He looks disheveled and dispirited.

What used to be stylish stubble on his face is now an unruly and scraggly start of a beard. His red-rimmed eyes are hollow nearly to the point of vacant. His pale skin is clammy and puffy.

He stumbles as he tries to walk over to me and nearly goes down.

"I came to try to help some more," he says, "but . . ."

I reach out and help hold him up.

"You need rest," I say. "When's the last time you ate?"

"Can't eat. Can't sleep. And I can't just sit at the house doing nothing. I can't."

I understand what he's saying and don't really know what to tell him or how to help him.

"Let me just stand here with you for a minute," he says.

"Why don't we sit down," I say, leading him over to

the picnic table.

When I have him situated on the bench, I grab a bottle of water from a nearby cooler and give it to him.

He opens it but doesn't drink.

"I can't believe she . . . right there in front of us," he says. "I . . . I was sure I could talk her out of it. I thought . . . if I just . . . had enough . . . time. If I could just get her to listen to me. But . . . then she just . . . right there with us . . . watching."

"I know. I'm so sorry."

"I really . . . didn't want them breaking up," he says. "Always thought they'd get married one day. She was so . . . wounded . . . but such a good person. They were good together. God, I can't believe they're both gone."

He breaks down and begins to cry again.

His eyes are so red I almost expect blood to fall from them.

It's all too much. The despair. The oppressive loss. The soul-crushing sadness.

We sit in silence for a long time, him sniffling beside me, search and rescue boats moving about in the river before us.

The relentless river. The pitiless, relentless river.

It takes a while, but eventually he runs out of tears.

From crying to sniffling to silence then to words again.

"Mean to ask you something," he says.

"What's that?"

"Did any of Shane's army buddies mention a Kayden Reynolds to you?"

"Kayden Reynolds," I repeat. "Why?"

"'Cause I've never heard of her before," he says.

236

"Yeah?"

"And she's listed as the beneficiary on his life insurance policy."

Chapter Forty-seven

They are beginning to find his offerings, starting to pro-
fane his sacred baptismal burials prior to the resurrection.

They can't even begin to imagine or appreciate what
they are disturbing and defiling.

Soon they will be knocking on his door. Soon they
will come for him.

He had always thought they might eventually, but
this is too quick, too soon. He's not ready. Not finished.

Why did this always happen to him? Why was he
always persecuted?

You know why, my son.

*If the world hate you, ye know that it hated me before it hated
you. If ye were of the world, the world would love his own, but because ye are not of the world, but I have chosen you out of the world,
therefore the world hateth you. Remember the word that I said unto
you, The servant is not greater than his lord. If they have persecuted
me, they will also persecute you.*

But it's not fair.

No, it's not.

It always happens to me. Always. My whole life. I've
always been the one. They've always had it in for me. Everyone. Always. Me. My whole life.

What do I do?

Present your body a living sacrifice, holy, acceptable unto God, which is your reasonable service.

I'm not ready.

Yes you are.

I need to make another sacrifice first. Need to atone. To prepare myself, to make my garments as white as snow.

Make your sacrifice. Prepare your soul. Make all things ready, for I come unto thee.

He looks out over the crowd.

People everywhere.

Pick one. Pick a pascal lamb from among the herd.

Everyone's moving. All the lights and noise. Blinking. Flashing. Spinning. Pounding music. Bass. Bass. Bass. Boom. Boom. Boom. Flash. Flash. Flash.

Look. Concentrate. Find her.

He scans the crowd more closely.

She's here. Find her.

Look. See.

All will be revealed.

And then there she is.

Stepping out of the smoke and lights and noise and movement. It's as if she's suddenly in a spotlight, everything else around her fading, dimming down to nothing.

Behold.

Behold the lamb.

Misty?

Like all the other sacrifices before her, at first he thinks she is Misty.

Misty. His little sister on the cross. The ultimate sacrifice. His foster dad handing him the crucifix for him to use on her.

Her being sacrificed to save him.

As the beautiful young girl who looks like Misty walks his way, he lifts the crucifix dangling from his neck, places it in his mouth, and begins to suck on it. His jeans tightening around his expanding erection.

When she smiles at him she looks even more like Misty.

Not that he needs it, but he receives even further confirmation when the glint of the cross around her neck catches his eye.

Behold. Behold the lamb. Behold Misty. Behold.

Are you ready?

I'm ready.

And when they come, I'll be ready. I'll make my body a living sacrifice and take the godless lot of sinners with me.

For his first act in his new vocation, I invite Merrill Monroe to speak at the first Black Lives Matter/Love Is the Answer program at the GCI chapel.

As expected, we get a huge turnout, and have to turn inmates who want to attend away—with the promise we will repeat the program for them the following day.

It's Merrill's first time speaking in front of a large audience and though it's not a great speech, it's a great first step for him in his new path and a powerfully positive program for the men who attend.

He has always slid between the speech of the street and the formal register of the educated with effortless ease. Tonight, though, he only speaks in a manner the men can relate to, and it is truly persuasive.

His passionate and poignant message includes many wise and thought-provoking and memorable moments, but the highlight for me is:

"The cops ain't our enemy. The system is flawed and biased against us, against the poorest of all races. But that ain't where we need to start. Don't get me wrong. We need to address it. We need to redress injustice everywhere. Eventually. But . . . way I see it, the way we really make a difference is for us to say and to mean and to live Black Lives Matter—to us. To us first and foremost. If we, as black people, don't value black lives first, how can we expect others to? How many of us, how many of you, are yelling Black Lives Matter but not treating them like they do? How many of you are sitting here today because you treated black lives—your own and others—like they really don't matter? Until you take responsibility for that, until we all take responsibility for each other, our call for black lives to matter ain't gonna have no credibility and no one will listen like they should. Gotta ask you somethin' else. And you ain't gonna like it. But how many unarmed, innocent black men have been gunned down 'cause of stupid shit and crimes you did with a gun that contributed to police paranoia and profiling? If black lives really matter to you, take responsibility for that, take responsibility for yourself, take responsibility for each other first."

Following the program, as the men are lining up at the front door to be escorted back to the dorms, Will, the gentle, young African-American man with dark skin and a gap between his teeth who had told me I couldn't be a cop and a chaplain, stepped up to me.

"I was wrong about you," he says. "Sorry for what I said and how I acted. We need you here."

Chapter Forty-eight

The pale pumpkin-colored moon is big and bright and low in the late-evening sky, its reflection mirrored on Julia's smooth surface.

The girls are asleep.

Anna and I are on our back porch holding hands and looking at the lake when the doorbell rings.

She lifts the baby monitor to her ear to see if the sound has awakened the angels as I jump up and step inside the house to answer it.

When I open the door, Sam is standing there with an evidence bag in her hand.

"Sorry," she says. "I tried calling but . . ."

"Come in. Phone's chargin'. We're out back. Join us. Whatcha drinkin'?"

"Whatta you got?"

"Red, white, or Bud Light."

"Nothing a wee bit stronger?"

"That's what I drink," I say.

Her expression says, *And?*

"Which is why we don't keep it in the house."

"Oh, sorry. Didn't know you were a friend of Bill W's."

"Good friends and glad you didn't know," I say. "Think that's a good sign."

"Bud Light," she says. "In a bottle if you've got it."

"Coming up."

I grab a Bud out of the fridge and follow her through the living room and out the partially open French doors onto the back porch.

"Sorry to crash," Sam says.

"Don't be," Anna says, standing to welcome her, towering over her as she does. "Happy to have you. Cheers."

They clink glass and bottle, Sam hands me the clear plastic evidence bag, and we all sit down.

"Sorry again about this morning," Sam says. "Feel so bad for that poor girl. Have they found her yet?"

"Not yet. What's this?"

"Recovered from inside one of the crossbars in Apalach," she says.

Inside the bag are two small pieces of green-sheathed electrical wire and a fragment of aluminum with tiny indentations in it.

"Know you're trying to figure out what the bars are from," she says. "Thought this might help."

"What is it?" Anna asks.

"Two small wires and a tiny piece of aluminum," I say.

"Two more bodies were found this evening," she says to Anna. "Like Tampa and Apalach, they appear to be the same as ours."

"Where?"

"That's the thing," she says. "One in Biscayne Bay—which is the other end of the state from us, and one not even in our state—a lake in Eufaula, Georgia."

"Our guy gets around," I say.

"He certainly does. So what's he doing in all those places? Besides abducting, raping, killing, and crucifying young girls?"

"What if he has or works for a moving company?" Anna says. "Said he was seen in a white delivery truck."

"*Damn*," Sam says. "That's good. I like that. That fits. Wow."

"Oh," I say, "you thought my girl was just another pretty face, didn't you?"

"Not at all. I just didn't know she was quite that quick."

"Give good head too," Anna says.

Sam laughs hard.

"Sorry to just blurt that out. Too much wine."

"Don't be," Sam says. "That's exactly like something I would say. It'd only be too far if you felt like you had to do a demonstration to prove it."

Merrick sits alone at his desk, his fingers floating atop the keyboard before him.

His heart is hurting. His head is full.

He's working on his "Battin' the Breeze" column, his editorial in the *Gulf County Breeze*.

He has a lot to say, but how can he convey what he feels he must without alienating his readers, his subscribers, his friends and family?

Taking in a deep breath, releasing it slowly, he begins—the fingers floating above the keyboard tapping rhythmically, as if it's a percussion instrument instead of the interface between his thoughts and the word processor.

"Battin' the Breeze"
By Merrick McKnight
One of the aspects of our small community I've always appreciated the most is its compassion, its sense of community. When someone is in need, we step up. We pitch in. We rally around.

When one among our small number passes from this life to the next one, the family he or she leaves behind is inundated with out-pourings of condolences in the form of food and visits and assistance. More food, in fact, than the family can actually eat. I know. It happened to me when I lost my wife and son.

That's who we are. That's what we do.

Or that's who I thought we were, what I thought we did.

But we have failed someone among us in need. We did not step up. We did not pitch in. We did not rally around.

Instead, we rallied against her.

We took to the barber shop and the coffee shop and the auto parts store and, this time too, to social media, and we spread rumors and innuendo and gossip about one of our own—a vulnerable teenage girl.

An innocent girl. A girl who should have received our compassion and understanding even if she hadn't been.

We failed someone in need.

Is that who we are now? Is that what we now do?

Post hate on social media platforms instead of practicing kindness in person?

Spread rumors instead of share concern?

Gossip instead of giving compassion?

Have we gotten to the place where we only show love and share kindnesses when someone dies?

I realize how seductive social media is. I know the feeling of anonymity and impunity we can feel when sitting alone in the dim light of our small screens.

I know how communal gossiping and sharing news about others among us can feel.

And in spite of seeing how well we practice this dark form of community, this small-minded form of small-town life, I still believe we're better than this. Or that we can be.

We let Megan Stripling down. Let's don't do the same to her mom or the kids swimming with Shane McMillan when he went missing, or anyone else among us ever again.

It's a commitment I'm making.

Will you join me?

Chapter Forty-nine

Recently I've been studying how the mind works in regard to enlightenment, inspiration, and problem solving.

I've learned that the key to breakthroughs in insight and answers is to fill the mind with as much information as possible, work on figuring it out, but then stop and do something else so that the subconscious can solve it. The lightning bolt and eureka moments don't happen in a vacuum, don't come out of nowhere. They are birthed out of the practice of study and observation and processing information and then letting go—going for a walk, doing another task, sleeping on it—and allowing the subconscious to do its brilliant best.

This is why I went to sleep with pictures of the crossbars and the evidence bag Sam had brought over on my chest and cascading down onto the floor beside the bed.

Thinking. Figuring. Reasoning. Connecting. Deducing.

Then sleeping.

Dreams seemingly unrelated to the problem of the cross. Seemingly random and unrelated to anything—including each other. The mysteries of the subconscious mind.

I wake the next morning and tell Anna, then Sam and Reggie by phone.

The fragment of aluminum is part of a light bulb socket, the wire what was left of what carried electricity to the socket. The metal bars are the lighted support braces of a Ferris wheel.

The high school football team had brought a carnival to town as part of a fundraiser. It took place the weekend prior to the Tupelo Festival. Amber had gone. I had seen pictures of her and Rain there on his phone.

"You slick son of a bitch," Sam says. "You smart fuckin' bastard. Wow."

"I bet we'll find that the carnival has traveled to every town where a body was found," I say. "And we'll need to drag the rivers, lakes, bays, and beaches of every town it has been to."

"Oh my God," she says. "There will be so many. There could be so many more poor girls on crosses in watery graves out there right now. Rotting."

"Not rotting. Not as far as he's concerned. Waiting for the resurrection."

You're so good at what you do," Anna says. "At both things you do for work. You're very good at other things too, but I'm just talking about work right now."

My eyes sting and I blink several times.

I've just gotten off the phone with Sam to find her looking at me lovingly.

We are still in bed and she is still ravishingly, devastatingly, sleepily sexy.

"Thank you," I say. "That's so . . . that means so much."

"Think of how many parents will have their young daughters come home because of you. Think about all the young girls who won't be raped and tortured and murdered."

I think about that very thing for a moment, praying it's the case.

My phone rings as I'm getting ready.

"Morning," Reggie says.

"Morning."

"Nice work on the crossbars," she says.

"Thanks. Sam's tracking down info on the carnival that was here weekend before last when Amber disappeared. Then we'll pay them a visit."

"Love having FDLE involved," she says. "Takes care of all the jurisdictional bullshit. Let me know what y'all find out and what you need. As soon as you have something, I'll help with the warrant."

"Will do."

"Heard back from the investigator who interviewed Kayden Reynolds."

I told her yesterday what Tommy told me about Kayden being the beneficiary of Shane's life insurance policy, and she'd had a detective with the Columbus Police Department interview her last night.

"Yeah?"

"Said she was so distraught he had a very difficult time getting anything out of her."

"Distraught?"

"In the extreme," she says. "Crying uncontrollably. Cussin' Shane one minute, saying she just wants him back the next."

"She wasn't anything like that when I saw her," I say. "She didn't even really seem sad."

"Delayed grief?" she asks.

"Could be," I say, "but . . . I don't know. Seems off."

"Maybe she was just trying to cock block his interview. Anyway, she has an alibi for when Shane went missing. He's gonna double check it, but it seems legit. For what it's worth, he said her grief seemed legit to him too. And he's a seasoned professional who expects everybody to be lying."

I think about it, trying to make the pieces fit, but am unable to do it.

"She said she and Shane had been together for quite a while, said they met right after he finished basic and have been together ever since. Says it was his idea to put her on his life insurance. Says she'll take a polygraph if we want her to. Says we wouldn't be suspicious if we knew the reason he just changed it recently."

"Let me guess," I say. "She's pregnant."

"Bingo. Give that man a prize. She also said that was the reason he came down here to break up with Megan face to face. Said he planned to marry her."

Chapter Fifty

I pick up Sam in Tallahassee and we hop on I-10 East toward I-75 South.

We are headed to Gibsonton, the carnival capital of the world, just below Tampa.

Ten miles south of Tampa, Gibsonton, Florida was once where carnies from circuses, carnivals, sideshows, and fairs wintered in the off season. In its golden age all carnie roads led to Gib-town. Back then it was said that carnies met twice—once on the road and once in Gibsonton.

Though not much is left of what was once called Freaktown, Gibsonton has always been and will always be a sanctuary for fading carnival culture. Human oddities and shocking sideshow attractions have all but disappeared in America—and with them Gibsonton's most famous freaks, the eight-and-a-half-foot Giant Al and his two-foot-tall wife, Jeanie; Grace McDaniels, the mule-faced woman; Dotty, the fat lady. Gone are the glory days when Gibsonton had the nation's only low post office counter to accommodate midgets, and of the famed Hilton sisters, the Siamese twins who operated a fruit stand.

But rusting remnants remain and occasionally you see a huge man in full clown costume riding his electric wheelchair to the grocery store.

"The whole thing is sketchy as fuck," Sam says. "The company is called Abiding Joy Amusements. Evidently it's some sort of Evangelical organization that employs at-risk young people and ex-offenders. Their website is just one page that says, 'Do you want a carnival to come to your town for a fundraiser for your church or school?' And has a form you fill out. There's no contact info. No phone number or email. Only an address in Gibsonton."

I shake my head. "Anna and I and the girls went to it when it was in town," I say. "It was small but fun. Seemed well run—clean, neat, up-to-date equipment."

"Reggie's following up with the athletic director at the high school who dealt with them, but the basic deal is, you provide the place and do the promotion, and they give your organization thirty percent of the profit."

"How'd he find them?"

"The football program where he was a coach before he came here had them in for a fundraiser. He remembered it being popular and raising a good bit of money for the program. Went online. Filled out the form. Had them here. They've traveled to everywhere we've found a victim so far. Won't be able to check everywhere they've been until we have more on them, but the website says they only travel in Florida, Alabama, and Georgia."

We are quiet a moment and I wonder how many bodies on crosses are in how many bodies of water in those three states.

"Think about the carnival coming to town," she says. "You don't know anything about them, but trust your kids' safety to them, eat their food, ride their portable pop-up rides."

"We give a lot of people and organizations like that our trust," I say. "Because we think someone is watching them, someone is making sure the food is good and the rides are safe, but like so many things in our country since the eighties when so much became deregulated, no one is really watching and no one does anything until there's a problem."

"By which time it's too late," she says. "Fuckin' greedy motherfuckers are poisoning our drinking water and tainting our meat and destroying the only planet we have, and their little lapdogs who are supposed to be our elected officials are giving them tax incentives to do it."

"You ever been to Gibsonton before?" I ask.

"As a kid," she says. "You?"

"Heard about it for a long time but've never been."

"Not much to it anymore," she says. "Just sort of the remains of what it once was. A special town for freakshow freaks, a place of acceptance and community for people like Percilla the Monkey Girl, Grady Stiles the Lobster Boy, and that couple billed as the weirdest in the world . . . what was . . . he was eight feet four and she was a two-foot-tall woman with no legs—Al Tomaini, I think. And Jeanie."

What remains of those people and the culture they were part of are memories, monuments, markers, and memorabilia. Which can also be said of the town itself.

My phone vibrates. It's Reggie.

"Where are y'all? How's it going?"

"Getting on 75," I say. "You find out anything else about the carnival?"

"Not yet. I'm calling to bounce something off of you."

"Okay."

"You know how all the crazy theories about Shane have been flying around?"

"Yeah?"

"What if they're not that farfetched after all?"

"Which?"

"The ones about somebody coming to take him out or about him faking his death to go AWOL?"

"I've been thinking about it," I say. "Might be something to it. Definitely don't want to ignore any possibilities—not until we have a body and know more."

"I'm wondering if we might not ought to broaden our investigation. Our search."

"Maybe," I say. "But—"

"We found a boot print farther up the path behind the houseboat," she says. "Like a military-style boot print."

I think about it.

"I was thinking . . ." she says, "if Shane faked his own death and wound up over there on that path, he'd be barefooted, so it's probably not his. But what if someone—like a mercenary or black ops . . . something like that—came down there to . . . take him out. They'd have those kinds of boots on."

"Lots of people wear boots on the river," I say. "Hunting boots, snake boots, work boots. They probably all leave a similar print."

"Sound crazy, don't I?"

"No. Not at all. We have to consider everything."

"You know I'd've never suggested anything like this if we'd've found his body. We just need to find his body."

"I know. How about Megan's?"

"Nothing yet. Hers too. We need to find them both. Okay. Letting you go now. Going to hang my head in shame for being so susceptible to wild theories and un-substantiated rumors. Appreciate it if you'd keep this just between us."

"You got it, boss."

"What was that about?" Sam asks.

"Nothing. I mean it amounted to nothing. Just Reggie wanting to make sure we don't think too narrowly about Shane's disappearance."

"Listen to this," she says, reading from her phone. "Lobster Boy was a violent little prick."

"What?" I say. "No. Say it ain't so."

"He was a bad alcoholic and used to beat the shit out of his family. He had a lot of upper body strength from the way he got around. He actually killed his oldest daughter's fiancé the night before their wedding. Admitted to it on the stand and was charged with third-degree murder, but because no prison at the time could accommodate an inmate with ectrodactyly, he was given probation instead. He stopped drinking during that time and remarried his first wife. But soon he was back to beating her and the kids again. Finally, he was shot and killed in 1992 when his wife and her son from a previous marriage hired a seventeen-year-old sideshow performer named Chris Wyant to kill Stiles for fifteen hundred bucks."

"Who knew the value of the life of Lobster Boy was so low," I say.

"Well, you gotta remember," she says, "fifteen hundred dollars was more back in '92."

Chapter Fifty-one

We drive around Gibsonton for a while, searching for but unable to find the address given for the headquarters of Abiding Joy Amusements.

Remnants of what it once was. Occasional. Random. Sporadic.

Rusting rides behind chain-link.

Ticket booths and animal cages and clown cars—colors fading, paint peeling, caving in, vine-covered.

Everything on wheels. Everything in trailers.

Semi-tractor-trailers with barely perceptible carnival logos. Rusted rims. Flat tires. No tires.

Rows and rows of dated and dilapidated attractions and amusements. Occasionally, a vibrantly colorful mostly plastic new one.

Yards with crumbling carousels in the front. Houses with leaning Ferris wheels rising above them from the backyard, their passenger cars tilted and tumbling.

"The zoning laws have always been lax here," Sam says. "Allowed all the amusement equipment and the raising of exotic animals right in residential areas."

After our third time of passing the International Independent Showmen's Museum, we realize we're not going to find what we're looking for with our wits and GPS.

"I don't want to," Sam says, "but we may need to stop and ask someone."

I pull into the Showtown Restaurant and Lounge and we get out.

"Probably should eat while we're here," she says.

"I'd feel better about getting it to go," I say.

She nods. "You're right.

Showtown—another name Gibsonton has gone by—is open and roomy with tables on one side and a bar on the other. Mixed in among the typical jukebox, pool tables, and karaoke setup are the more exotic humorous character paintings and elaborate murals.

Because Sam is so slight, I feel funny and a little self-conscious walking into the joint with her, and I wonder if we in any way resemble the giant Al Tomaini and his half-woman wife, Jeanie.

We order—her a BLT, me a black and blue burger—and begin to ask around about Abiding Joy Amusements.

No one has heard of it. And no one recognizes the address. Until the oldest active showman in the country walks in wearing a dated brown suit, bolero, cowboy boots, and hat.

"Operates under a lot of different names," he says. "That's not one that is displayed anywhere. Big family. The Banks. Willard and Brenda Banks. Old crazy coots that got religion. Bunch of foster kids I believe. Keep to themselves. No one new around here would know them."

"Can you tell us how to get there?" Sam says.

"Sure, but they're not there. They're on the road."

"Do you know where?" I ask.

"No, but Willard's mother lives across the street

from them. She will."

Chapter Fifty-two

When we pull up I know we're at the right place.

"This is it," I say.

Sam nods. "I think so too."

It looks more like a compound than a residence.

Tall wood-slat fence backed by chain-link around the entirety of the property—five acres or more.

Overgrown. Oppressive. Unwelcoming. All accentuated by the gray clouds gathering.

"Hiding from the world, isn't it?" Sam says.

Huge oak trees, draped heavily with Spanish moss, shade and shelter what takes place here.

Beyond an out of place wrought iron gate with two huge crucifixes on it, a dirt-road driveway leads to a grouping of buildings centered around an old Victorian home in need of repair and painting.

The gate is partially open, ajar perhaps just enough for us to pull through.

As I slowly drive through the opening, Sam says, "I can't help but feel like we're crossing over into something, some . . . I don't know. An almost mythical . . . dimension."

"We're leaving our world and entering his," I say.

A low rolling thunder rumbles in the dark distance.

Like many of the other places we've seen in Gibsonton today, amusement equipment, rides, trucks, and trailers are spread about, haphazardly scattered around the property. Most of them with tall grass in need of cutting beneath and right around them.

In a clearing to our right, a huge swinging pirate ship built onto a flatbed trailer looks lost at sea.

"Look at those," Sam says, pointing over the dashboard to what is rising above the big, asymmetrical house.

The tops of different size Ferris wheels can be seen over the steep, multi-facing rooftops and towers.

Small mostly wooden buildings are spread about, and near the main house there are other smaller houses with similar architecture so that they appear to be miniature version of the centerpiece.

The place appears abandoned. No sign that anyone is here or has been in quite some time.

I continue around the main house to the back.

When we get there it's not the standing Ferris wheels but the one lying on the ground that grabs my attention.

No base or stand. No passenger cars. Only the wheel. Only part of the wheel. Not much more than a frame missing support bars, broken bulbs and white paint chipping off the ones that remain.

"Oh God, John," she says. "It's huge and there are a lot of crossbars missing."

I frown and nod and think of all the horror that reality represents.

In the rearview mirror, I see an emaciated-looking elderly lady appear in the back doorway.

A simple white-cotton sheath dress covers her narrow frame and a large crucifix hangs from her neck to dangle between her braless breasts, the erect nipples of which poke through thin fabric. Atop her small head is a shock of gray hair spreading out in every direction, standing on end as if she's just been electrocuted.

I put the car in Park and we get out.

"What're you doin' here?" she says. "Whatta you want?"

We're both holding our badges up and identifying ourselves before she's even finished with her questions.

"Who are you, ma'am?" Sam says.

"Mrs. Mary Francis Banks."

"Do you live here?"

"I live across the street," she says. "This is my son's place. Came over to feed the animals. He's not home right now."

"What's his name?"

"Willard Banks. What's this about?"

"Where is he?" I ask.

"Working. They all are."

"Where?"

"Don't know, but they'll be home late tonight, so somewhere pretty close probably. I'd have to look to be sure," she says. "And you'd have to tell me what this is about, to get me to do that."

"How old is Willard?" I ask.

"Sixty-four. Be sixty-five next month."

"How many young men does he employ?" Sam says.

"He's got mostly girls, but there's Bobby Lee."

"Bobby Lee?"

"Well, Robert, but everybody calls him Bobby Lee. Bobby Lee Banks. Call him the quiet one too. He's kinda shy and soft spoken, when he speaks at all. He's adopted."

Sam looks at me, her eyes widening a moment.

"How old is he?" she asks.

"Not positive. Twenty-four maybe."

"He ever work on this Ferris wheel on the ground here?" I ask.

She looks over at it and nods. "Taking it apart. Taking his time doing it, you ask me."

"Where's he live?" Sam says.

"What's all this about? Something happened? Is he okay?"

"Where does he live?" Sam says again, her voice growing more stern.

"Used to live here in the main house, now has the first little cottage round the front on the right."

"What's he drive?" I ask.

"Drive? He been in some sort of accident? Don't know why he insists on driving that big truck around everywhere."

"What does he drive?" I say again, more slowly.

"A truck. I just told you."

"What kind? What color?"

"GMC I think. White. Boxy in the back. Like a moving truck. What's going on?"

"We just want to make sure everyone is okay," Sam says, her voice soft and soothing again. "Let's look at the schedule and find out where they are, okay?"

Chapter Fifty-three

Emergency lights flashing, we are racing up FL 60 toward Crystal River.

Our nerves jangling with energy like high tension lines.

Up ahead of us the sky is dark. Banks of storm heads building. Low thunder rumbling. Lightning flashing occasionally.

Sam is on the phone, the printout of Abiding Joy Amusements' itinerary in her lap, a big red circle around Crystal River on it.

She is working on warrants and backup and the co-ordination of local agencies both in Gibsonton and Crystal River. With statewide jurisdiction, FDLE can pull warrants anywhere in Florida, but usually involves local agencies in the process.

I am on the phone with Reggie, filling her in, letting her know what we found, what we have, what we're doing.

As soon as the warrants are issued, the Hillsborough County Sheriff's Department will execute them on the Bankses' property and FDLE crime scene techs will take the place apart.

As much as we'd like to be there for that, the more

pressing matter is the apprehension of Bobby Lee Banks with the help of the Citrus County Sheriff's Department near Crystal River.

"Great work, John," Reggie is saying.

"We don't have him yet."

"And be careful getting him," she says. "He's dangerous and will be desperate. Do what you've got to do to get him, but stay safe doing it."

When I finish talking to Reggie, I call Anna.

Sam is still on the phone and is going to be for a while.

I tell her what's going on and then talk to Johanna.

"Hey sweet girl," I say. "Are you having a good day?"

"I am. Are you, Daddy?"

The first of the raindrops begin to pepper the car.

"It's a lot better now, just hearing your voice. What have you been doing?"

"We . . . ah . . . let's see . . . went for a walk."

"Yeah? How was that?"

"Nice but hot. Then we made cookies and I colored and Miss . . ." She turns her mouth away from the phone. "Anna, what's the lady who . . . Oh, yeah. Miss Michelle came over and me and Taylor watched a video while they talked."

"That does sound like a good day," I say. "A very good day."

"When will you be home, Daddy? I miss you."

"Just as soon as I can, but it will be later tonight. I miss you too. Can't wait to see you."

"If I'm asleep, will you wake me up, Daddy?"

"I will. I'm gonna need a hug and a kiss."

"Me too."

"Bye sweet girl. I love you. I'm so proud of what a good, kind girl you are."

"Bye bye, Daddy. Love you too."

She hands the phone back to Anna.

The rain intensifies, the day darkens. Across the median, headlights come on. Up ahead of us, red driving lights and brighter brake lights glow against the gray.

"Michelle came over?" I say.

"Yeah. Said she had to get out of the house. She's really struggling. Heartbroken about Shane but just so upset for Tommy too. We talked about the four of us going away somewhere for the weekend in the near future."

"Sounds good."

"Are you okay?" Anna asks.

"Yeah," I say.

"You don't sound like it."

"Sorry. Just tired."

She has picked up on the sense of dread and foreboding I feel—something I doubt anyone else would have.

The rain is coming harder now, and I turn up the wipers as I back off the accelerator some.

"It's more than that," she says. "What is it? Has something happened you're not telling me about? Are you hurt?"

"No. Nothing like that."

"Can you tell me?"

I glance over at Sam. She is focused intently on her conversation about the importance of processing Bobby Lee Banks's house and the old Ferris wheel the right way.

The wipers sling water side to side, but the moment they do, more rain sluices down the glass, smearing the colors seen through it, blurring the dim objects before us even more.

"Just a new experience for me," I say.

"What is?"

I lower my voice. "Going into a situation like this now that I have you and our girls."

"Oh."

"I'm . . . I feel . . . more vulnerable. Like I have more at stake . . . more . . . to lose."

"You do," she says. "And we do too. So be extra careful."

"I will."

"But not so careful or overly cautious you hesitate or second-guess yourself."

Just talking to her makes me feel better, less tight, less fearful.

"We're going to be praying for you," she says. "And we can't wait until you come home to us tonight. Just make sure you do. That's what matters most. Tell me you'll see me later tonight. Promise me you will."

Chapter Fifty-four

Located in the heart of Florida's Nature Coast, Crystal River is a small town of around three thousand people about sixty miles north of Tampa.

Known as the home of the manatee, the Crystal River community surrounds Kings Bay—the spring-fed body of water home to some four hundred manatees during the winter, when the Gulf of Mexico cools.

At one time, Crystal River was known as Weewahiiaca—a Creek word combining *wewa*, meaning water, with *haiyayaka*, meaning clear.

Clusters of warm springs feed the area with millions of gallons of crystal clear water every day.

Crystal River itself—the river not the town—is a short river that flows the seven miles from Kings Bay to empty into the Gulf of Mexico.

The carnival is set up in an empty lot near a baseball field not far from the high school.

It rained earlier and everything is still wet, drops of water refracting all the bright blinking lights of amusement rides and food vendors.

We meet members of the Citrus County Sheriff's Department a few blocks away to coordinate our approach, and when we enter the carnival, we go in quietly with deputies posted at every exit.

No lights. No sirens. No show.

Music pounding. Bass thumping. The *click clack* of track. The mechanical whirs of machinery, the blasts of air from hydraulics.

The yells and screams and laughs and loud chatter of young people having a good time.

The smells of vendor food—the char of grilling meat, the butter of popcorn, the sugar of cotton candy and candied apples.

And everywhere movement. Amusement rides spinning, swinging, turning, tilting, falling, rising. People walking. Children running. Throwing softballs and darts and shooting basketballs.

It's nearly dark as we enter the front gate, show our badges, and ask where Robert Lee Banks is.

"Bobby Lee? The big Ferris wheel in the back," the young blonde with abnormally large green eyes in the ticket booth says. "Is everything okay? You want to talk to my dad?"

"Your dad named Willard Banks?" Sam asks.

"Yes ma'am."

"Where is he?"

"Walking around checking on things probably. I can radio him."

"Tell you what, don't bother him. We'll be back in a few minutes and then we'll have you call him up here for us, okay?"

"Yes, ma'am."

We make our way through the throng of people, weaving around rides and the long lines of people patiently waiting to ride them.

All about us the whir of spinning machines, the blur of streaking lights.

The competing sounds. The overstimulation. The dance of human beings interacting with each other and apparatuses designed specifically for their amusement.

As we near the huge Ferris wheel in the back, a trim middle-aged man with closely cropped gray hair, the gaunt look of a drunk, and severe dark eyes steps out of the crowd, extends his hand, and says, "I'm Willard Banks. Heard you were looking for me. How can I help?"

"We'll have some questions for you in a minute," Sam says, "but right now we're looking for your son, Bobby Lee."

We continue toward the Ferris wheel.

"What's this about?" he says, turning to try to keep up with us.

"Just have some questions for him," she says.

"Okay. No problem. Right over here."

We reach the Ferris wheel to find a shy, simple-looking teenage girl with brown hair operating it.

"Where's your brother?" Willard asks.

She looks confused. "Which one?"

"The one who's supposed to be operating this ride," he says. "Bobby Lee."

She shrugs. "He left. Just told me to run this until he got back."

"How long ago?" I ask.

"Fifteen, twenty minutes, maybe."

"Where'd he go? Did he leave the grounds?"

Chapter Fifty-five

A BOLO is issued for a white GMC delivery truck with no markings, and we are racing toward the river on the lookout for it.

An investigator with the Citrus County Sheriff's Department is interviewing members of the Banks family for general information, waiting for Sam and me to conduct the more in-depth interviews relating to the murders.

Every deputy available is searching the area for Bobby Lee Banks, his white delivery truck, and Leslie Marie Boning, who appears to have gone missing from the carnival tonight.

I'm driving faster than I should be. Beside me, Sam is on the phone trying to figure out the most likely place Bobby Lee would take his latest abductee.

She ends her call and checks her texts. "Oh my God," she says. "Look at this."

She holds the phone over to me and I take a quick glance at it.

A selfie of a young blonde girl fills the screen.

"Is that Leslie Marie?" I say.

She nods. "Could be Amber's sister, couldn't she?" She looks at something else, then adds, "Or his. Look at this."

I again glance at the phone in her outstretched hand.

The scanned picture is much older but the similarities to the other girls is striking.

"Who's that?"

"Bobby Lee's little sister. Died years ago in a horrible freak accident while being baptized in a lake at church camp."

I shake my head as I wonder how many other of the young girls who had died since then were directly related to what happened to her.

The blue lights behind the grill of my Impala are flashing, refracting off the wet pavement. In the far, dark distance—both through my windshield and in my rearview mirror—I see similar lights atop patrol cars flashing against the blackness.

Sam's phone rings—something it's been doing nearly nonstop.

"It's Daniel," she says. "I called him earlier and missed him. I can call him back after we—"

"No," I say. "Take it. Talk to him."

"Thanks," she says, and pats my arm gently.

I glance over and smile at her.

"Hello, husband," she says, her voice playful and loving. "It's okay. I was just calling to check in and tell you I love you, but we're in the middle of a . . . thing right now. Can I call you back later? . . . Love you too. . . . I will. . . . Uh huh. . . . Be back just as soon as I can."

She hangs up and I say, "Aren't you glad you took his call?"

"Yes. Thanks. He's . . . such a good husband. I'm very lucky."

"You both are."

"So are you and Anna. Marital bliss isn't as rare as people make out, is it?"

"No," I say, "but rare enough to hold on to and be grateful for when you find it."

She nods. "No doubt. Stay on this road another half mile or so . . . then take River Camp Road on your right. It's a dirt road. If Bobby Lee's been staking this place out, he's likely to go to the landing somewhere around here."

In less than a minute, we veer off the paved highway onto River Camp Road.

"Should dead end into it," she says.

"How far?"

"No idea. Can't be too far. We're already close to the river."

"Search down every side road, path, and pig trail we pass," I say. "He may—"

I slam on the breaks as we come to a single bar gate chained and locked, undisturbed.

"Doesn't look like anyone's been through here in a while," Sam says.

I'm already backing up.

Finding a place to turn around, I race back to the road, pull back onto it, and head in the same direction.

The road is empty.

No oncoming cars or emergency lights to fight against the night.

Only our white headlights and blue flashers in the front, our red driving lights in the back against the damp darkness of the desolate rural road.

"Should be another one a little ways up," Sam says, then adds with an adorable smile, "Quit driving like a girl and get us there."

I laugh.

"We're about to get him," she says. "And that'll be that. And . . ."

"What?"

"I . . . I'm gonna miss working with you," she says.

"Me too."

"See that reflector?" she says. "That's it."

I slow a little, but not enough to get mocked, and sling the car onto the side road, fishtailing and slinging damp, clumpy dirt into the ditch.

"That's more like it," she says.

We race down the narrow, overgrown dirt road, the car bouncing hard over holes and ruts, knocking it out of alignment if not doing more serious damage.

"There," she says. "Look."

I lock up the brakes and we skid to a stop.

"Back up," she says.

But before I can, she's jumping out of the car and running toward the little side road we just passed.

"Sam. Wait."

She keeps moving.

I throw the car in reverse and back up fifteen feet or so to an even smaller, more narrow side road and turn onto it, my headlights illuminating Sam, the blue of the flashers splashing the back of the white truck she's racing toward.

The truck is parked down an overgrown dirt path, the branches of the oak tree canopy covering the top few feet of its big boxy back end.

I pull up behind her, but by the time I reach her, she is already shoving up the back cargo door.

"POLICE," she yells. "DON'T MOVE."

Her gun is drawn and she wisely stands to the side.

When the door rolls up, it reveals Bobby Lee Banks standing on the killing floor of his mobile torture chamber.

Beneath the mounted metal crucifixes, what looks like an operating theater is brightly lit.

A young, blonde, naked girl is strapped to an old-fashioned exam table, legs up, feet cuffed into stirrups.

Jamming the car into Park, I jump out, removing my Glock from its holster as I do.

"NO. NO. NO," Bobby Lee yells. "NO. NOT YET. I'M NOT READY."

"Drop the knife, Bobby Lee," she says.

Coming up the other side, I point my gun at Bobby Lee's disturbed and demented head. "We've got you," I say. "Up to you whether you want to go in alive or dead."

"Drop the knife," Sam says. "NOW."

"Okay, okay," he says.

He places the knife on a stainless steel tray beside him.

"Don't shoot," he says. "I put it down. Okay? I did what you said, so—"

He grabs a gun from the tray and starts firing, rounds ricocheting off the metal bed of the truck, pocking the equipment, piercing the windshield of my car.

Sam and I both return fire.

I have the cleaner shot. Hers has to come through equipment and the table with the girl on it.

I squeeze off a single round. Wait. Aim again, adjusting for his movement. Then squeeze off a second.

He goes down, dropping his gun as he does.

Besides twitching a bit, he doesn't move.

My ears ring from the gunfire and I feel the slight disequilibrium from the partial deafness.

On the table, Leslie Marie moves. Not much. But enough to let us know she's alive.

"You're gonna be okay, Leslie," Sam says. "We're here now. You're going to be fine."

My weapon is still aimed at the unmoving Bobby Lee as Sam holsters hers and moves over toward me.

"Pretty sure it was my round that put him down," she says with a smile.

I smile back at her, realizing just how much I'm going to miss her, just how happy I am in this moment to get this killer with her.

She starts climbing up into the back of the truck when we hear a door up front open.

"Uncle Bobby?" a child's voice says. "Is everything okay?"

"Oh my God," Sam says. "He's got a child with him."

"It's okay," she says. "We're the police. Just stay where you are."

She climbs back down. "You check on her," she says. "I'll take care of the kid."

Keeping my weapon trained on the still unmoving Bobby Lee, I awkwardly begin climbing up into the truck.

I see movement out of the corner of my eye and glance back to see the kid—an eleven-year-old boy—rounding the corner.

"Stay there, sweetheart," Sam says. "Don't come any closer."

She moves toward him, not much bigger than he is, holding her hands up, trying to keep him from seeing what's inside the truck, when he brings up a small revolver and shoots her at pointblank range.

Chapter Fifty-six

Though she won't remember, I keep my promise to Johanna and wake her for a hug and kiss when I finally get home.

Long after she's fallen back asleep, I sit there holding her—holding her and praying over her and caressing her hair and kissing her head.

After risking waking Taylor because I couldn't not kiss her too, I meet Anna in the sanctuary of our bed.

Without uttering a single word, she comforts me more than anything can.

Holding me, caressing my skin, kissing my head, she begins the process of healing for me.

Then come the words.

We talk for hours, past the point that night turns into day.

She asks the right questions. Says the right things. Listens so intently. Let's me both express and process everything I need to.

Eventually I am able to make love. Eventually I am able to sleep.

In my dream, I'm shooting and killing the kid who has just shot Sam over and over. The whole nightmare is on a loop that I can't get to stop.

Him shooting Sam.

Her falling.

Me turning and firing. Instantly. Automatically. Reflexively.

A huge hole opening in the center of his chest, blood oozing out, staining his white T-shirt crimson and black.

Over and over and over. Me killing a kid.

Bang.

Bang-BANG.

In the dream I'm aware it's on a loop, but no matter what I do I can't jump off the giant, incessantly turning Ferris wheel of it.

When I wake, I hear Anna talking very softly.

She is on the phone, obviously trying not to wake me.

I blink my eyes open, having no idea what time it is.

I reach for my phone on the bedside table to check the time. It's dead. I completely forgot to plug it in last night.

"He's awake," Anna says. "Here. It's Reggie."

She hands me the phone.

"Sorry," I say. "Forgot to plug in my phone last night."

"I wasn't going to call, but . . . I wouldn't have if . . ."

"What is it?"

"Search and rescue recovered Megan's body late last

night and they found Shane's just now," she says.

"I'm on my way."

I hand Anna her phone and kiss her forehead.

"I've got to go to the landing," I say, "but then I'm coming back and we're going to have breakfast and then spend the entire day together. Just the four of us. And we're all going to take a long nap this afternoon. And then go out to dinner tonight. Just us."

"Sounds heavenly," she says, stretching, it changing her voice. "Hurry back."

Chapter Fifty-seven

Together in death, Shane and Megan lie next to each other on the wide-bottom boat, their hands actually touching as if they're reaching for one another.

Given the circumstances—her gunshot wound to the head and his length of time in the water—they both look remarkably well.

The river had washed away all the blood and brain matter from Megan's face, neck, and head. The hole beneath her chin is small and the flap of skin on her scalp is lying down, and she looks to be taking a nap after getting out of the pool on a pleasant summer morning.

Though he shouldn't, Shane looks even better than Megan—with one exception. He has some faint purplish bruising by his right eye and around his neck.

It's a week to the day since he went into the water, but he certainly doesn't appear to have been in nearly that long.

When the ME turns him over, his back and the backs of his legs have the dark purple patches of fixed lividity.

"**A**sk any medical examiner or coroner in the country," the ME is saying. "Drownings are the most difficult when it comes to determining cause of death and whether it was homicide, accident, or suicide. Hands down the hardest."

"But—" Reggie begins.

"We'll do a full autopsy," he says, holding up his hands in a placating gesture, "and we'll rush it for you, but I'm just telling you . . . don't expect too much."

Drownings are almost always accidental. And he's right, determining the manner of death is extremely difficult—often a process of exclusion, the ME beginning by ruling out what *didn't* happen. Even the finding of pulmonary edema, water in the lungs, doesn't actually prove drowning because it can occur in deaths from heart attacks and overdoses.

"We understand," I say, "but doesn't the male victim look too good to have been in this warm river water for a week?"

"We don't get to speculate on stuff like that," he says. "That's your job. I don't mean . . . I mean that in a good way. You get to speculate and theorize and deduce. All we get to do is tell you what the science says and what's likely based on it."

"If you hadn't been told the male had gone under a week ago," I say, "how long would you estimate he'd been in the water?"

"Less time than that."

Tommy and Michelle are waiting for us when we get back to the landing.

280

Thankfully, it's just me, Reggie, and Ralph. The boat with the bodies went to a lower landing to meet the funeral home that is going to transport the bodies.

"Is it him?" Tommy asks as we walk toward them.

All three of us nod.

They both begin to cry, each reaching out to the other for support.

"We found Megan too," Ralph says.

"That's . . . good," Tommy says. "That's . . . Ordinarily, they'd ask me to do her funeral, but . . . under the circumstances . . ."

"Maybe they still will," Michelle says. "I'm just so relieved we have them both back. I was beginning to think we might not ever find them."

Tommy looks at Ralph. "Thank you. And please thank your entire team for all their tireless effort and hard work on our behalf. We are truly grateful. It's such a relief to be able to have a funeral and actually bury him. Such a relief."

"And thank you two for all you've done," Michelle says to me and Reggie.

"Yes. Absolutely," Tommy adds. "I didn't mean to leave you two out. I'm just—"

"We know," I say.

"But we're not the ones who found them," Reggie says. "That's Ralph and his team."

"Did he . . ." Tommy begins. "Just . . . was it . . . does it look like it was . . . just an accident?"

Michelle says, "Megan and the other boys or that Bobby Lee Banks didn't have anything to do with it, did they?"

"We'll know more after the autopsy," I say. "Acciden-

281

tal drowning is still most likely, but we won't know for sure until we get everything back."

They nod as more tears stream down their cheeks.

"We heard what happened down in Crystal River," Tommy says to me. "So, so sorry. I should've called you when I heard, but . . . I've just been . . . so . . . but things are going to get better now. Now that we have him back. If you need anything . . . please call me."

"I will and you do the same."

"Maybe," Michelle says, "we can all help each other heal."

I return home and crawl back into bed beside Anna.

When I wake again, I am alone.

Stumbling down the hallway, I can hear my three girls interacting in the kitchen.

"Who's ready for breakfast?" I say.

"Daddy!" Johanna squeals.

She runs over to me and I pick her up and hug her for a long moment.

"Finding breakfast might be a bit of a challenge," Anna says. "It's almost three in the afternoon."

"Who's ready for lunch?" I say.

"We already had lunch, silly," Johanna says.

"Who's ready for dinner?" I say.

"We're ready for whatever you want," Anna says. "What would you like?"

"Just to be with my girls."

I can tell Johanna is ready to get down and return to what she was doing, so I ease her down and step over and kiss Taylor on the top of her tiny head. She smells so good, of new skin and gentle baby shampoo, that I linger and kiss her some more.

"But you need to eat," she says. "When's the last time you did?"

"I had part of a black and blue burger for lunch in Gibsonton yesterday."

"Tell you what," she says. "Why don't we ride into Panama City and go to Waffle House and you get breakfast, lunch, and dinner?"

Chapter Fifty-eight

The next day, Anna and I leave Taylor with her aunt and take Johanna to Eufaula to meet Susan.

Susan seems better than she was, and the exchange, while heartbreakingly difficult, goes about as well as can be expected.

"We can make this work," I say to Susan.

She nods. "We will."

As he has continually been, the eleven-year-old kid with the gun flashes in my mind again. Sam being shot. Going down. The kid turning the gun toward me. Both of us firing.

A child. Just a child.

"It's just . . ." I say. "I've seen what happens when kids aren't . . ."

"Hey," she says. "Johanna's gonna be fine. We are too. It'll all work out. Promise."

After leaving Eufaula, we drive to Gainesville to Shands Hospital to see Sam.

We find Daniel at her bedside, touching and talking

to her though she is in a coma and not expected to come out of it.

"Look who it is, honey." Daniel says. "John and Anna drove all the way down to see you."

"Hey partner," I say.

She looks so small, pale, and frail lying in the bed, her blond hair flat and matted—the side where she was shot shaved, its swollen skin iodine-orange.

"You look so good," Anna says. "We'll be drinking wine on our back porch again in no time. Only this time you'll have to bring this handsome husband of yours and we'll grill some steaks. He'll be ready for some after all this hospital food."

"Yes, I will," Daniel says, his voice cracking. "I certainly will."

"We were talking in the car," I say. "Sam and I. On the way to . . . toward Crystal River. And we were talking about how marital satisfaction isn't as rare as some people make it out to be, talking about how lucky we were—me to have Anna and her to have you. It was one of the last things she said to me—what a great husband you are, Daniel."

We visit for a while and then stay with Sam while Daniel goes to get food and a few things he needs.

I am so glad Sam is here at Shands—and not just because of the quality of care, but because the young Banks boy I shot is in the hospital down near Tampa where they first took her. And though Leslie Marie Boning, the girl Bobby Lee had in his truck, is too, and I'd really like to check in on her, I'd find it very difficult to be that close to the boy again—or chance running into his family.

When Daniel comes back, Reggie and Merrick are

with him.

"Look who I found loitering out in the hallway," Daniel says.

"Didn't know y'all were coming," I say. "We could've ridden down together."

"I should've checked with you," Reggie says. "But I knew you were taking Johanna to meet her mother so . . . I didn't figure you were coming down here too."

"Couldn't not," I say.

"That really means a lot," Daniel says. "Really. You have no idea."

"We all love Sam," Anna says.

"And though we don't want to rush you," Reggie says to Sam, "we are anxious for you to come back to work."

At that, tears begin streaming down Daniel's cheeks.

Merrick, who is closest to him, puts his arm around him.

"She's got to get better," Daniel says. "Got to. I can't . . ."

We are all quiet a moment, and I reach down and take Sam's hand and begin to pray for her.

"Did she ever tell y'all how we met?" Daniel says. "She suspected me of being a serial killer."

"**T**here's a statewide task force for finding Bobby Lee Banks's victims," Reggie is saying.

We are standing out in the hospital hallway not from Sam's room.

It's just the two of us. Anna, Merrick, and Daniel are still inside with Sam.

"They're dragging large bodies of water in towns where the carnival is known to have gone. Our own search and rescue will be helping. Found two more so far. One in Pompano Beach. One in Sarasota."

I nod.

"We're hoping DNA from the truck will give us some indication on how many victims we're looking for, but for now we're looking at missing girls who match the profile from the places the carnival traveled to."

"He didn't just start when he got that truck and turned it into . . . what he turned it into."

"No. You're right. It's just a place to start. Some of the Banks foster kids are cooperating. Willard and his wife are pretending to be, but . . . they couldn't have been as oblivious as they claim. Ironically, it seems what they most wanted from the kids they took in was free labor. The real damage was done to Bobby Lee long before they adopted him. Couple of pretty sick foster monsters really did a number on him. Had a little sister die back then, which is why he was taken away from them. Now it looks like he may have been involved in killing her."

"Any update on Leslie Marie and the Banks kid?"

"The girl went home this morning," she says. "Y'all got to her before he had done much. She's traumatized, still in shock, but she's gonna be great again—and she has you to thank for that. You and Sam." She frowns as she glances back toward Sam's room. "The kid's gonna live. And I'm only glad about that for your sake. Bobby Lee used to force different young foster boys to go with him. Always armed. Always waiting in the front of the truck as a lookout. We've found two men so far we're pretty sure they shot—a fisherman near Bristol and a homeless man in Deerfield Beach.

The kid you shot is a hardened, fucked-up little monster in the making who had just killed a cop, and don't you forget it."

"Killed?" I say.

She nods. "From what I understand, Sam's not going to even wake up again and if she did, she'd be so brain damaged she could barely function."

Chapter Fifty-nine

Two days later, at his request, I am in the Gulf County Jail visiting Cody.

"I've got information," he says. "Can you get me a deal?"

"What do you have? Information about what?"

"Something you need to know before you rule Shane's death an accident."

"We're not about to rule Shane's death an accident."

"Can you help me or not?"

"Until I know what you have, I have no idea."

"If what I tell you is good," he says. "If it's helpful—whether it leads to an arrest or not, will you put in a word for me with the DA?"

I nod.

"Want to hear you say it," he says.

"I will. I will let them know of your cooperation throughout the investigation and if whatever you have now is relevant I'll let them know."

He nods. "Okay. I'm trusting you. Swolle and Shane were really jawing at each other. I mean really going at it. Almost came to blows."

"About?"

"A girl. Swolle kept calling him a punk-ass bitch, said he wasn't doing her right."

"Megan?"

"No. He was sayin' he should have been done with Megan a long time ago. He's talkin' 'bout this other girl. Said he was dissin' her. Was he hidin' her? Ashamed of her? Was he the racist asshole he'd always thought he was? Why wouldn't he bring her to town? Shit like that."

"Did you see Swolle do anything to Shane?"

"No, not exactly, but I's exhausted from the race and wasn't watching what was going on down there after I got out."

I nod.

So far he hasn't told me anything we didn't already know or suspect.

"Think about this shit," he says. "Shane's dead. Megan's dead. I'm locked up. Matt's locked up. The only one scot-fucking-free is Swolle's big black ass. Ask yourself why."

"I will. Thanks."

"Wait. I ain't even got to the part where I tell you what will get me some consideration."

"Okay."

"Shane had this thing for black girls. Liked young, thick, big-booty black girls. They was his thing, you know?"

"Yeah, we heard something like that."

"Well, he's got one—*had* one—a big-booty black girl up in Columbus, and she's pregnant with his baby."

I nod.

"Oh," he says. "You already knew that. Well, did you know that Swolle introduced them? Did you know she's his cousin?"

Later that afternoon, as I'm getting into my car to go home for the day, I get a courtesy call from the medical examiner and everything falls into place.

I know it's a courtesy call because he tells me so. Though he's actually returning my calls.

"Drownings are difficult," he says. "But I can say with relative certainty that the victim did drown. He was on his back long enough for lividity to become fixed there. There is bruising around his neck consistent with him being choked or held beneath the water."

"So it's homicide?"

"If it had been a gator I'd expect to see punctures in the skin, teeth or bite marks. Nothing like that is present."

"How about time of death?" I ask.

"Impossible to be very accurate," he says. "Best guess would be twenty-four to forty-eight hours before the body was recovered."

So Shane had only died a day or two before he was found. So where was he during those other five or six days? What was he doing? Who was he with? And who killed him five days after he was supposed to already be dead?

"We found no alcohol or drugs in his bloodstream," he says. "And his last meal, which hadn't fully digested yet, was hamburger steak, mashed potatoes, creamed corn, and collard greens."

I think of Sweet Willy's Soul Food Station.

"Final thing of consequence," he says. "We found chlorine in the water in his lungs and none of the river debris normally in victims who drown in a river. Finally, we found traces of Melia azedarach and its fruit in his lungs. The fruit is poisonous but there wasn't enough in him to hurt him, let alone kill him. It's only notable because they don't grow around the area where the victim was said to have gone missing or where the body was discovered."

"Melia azedarach?" I ask.

"Chinaberry tree."

When I don't respond, he says, "John? You there?"

I think of the sexy Kayden and her long, caramel legs and the filthy pool she had put them in, the pool surrounded by chinaberry trees and full of their residue and fruit, and I know where Shane was killed.

Chapter Sixty

"What I want to know is if you went there to kill him or if it was more of an impulsive act?" I say.

No response.

"Shane decides to fake his own death and vanish," I say. "You figured that out too, right? He had a pregnant girlfriend and they could live off the insurance money she would receive. Was that his only motivation or did it also have something to do with Carl's death? The Ranger who died in the Airborne accident? Probably both and maybe several things we'll never know. But he decided to do it and it sealed his fate."

Deadpan. Despondent. Implacable. Unreadable.

"When I talked to Kayden she wasn't even upset," I say. "But when the Muscogee County sheriff's investigator interviewed her she was so distraught she could hardly talk. I think because when I was there, Shane was too. He was alive. He was inside her trailer—which is why she acted like she was going out to get in that nasty pool when I walked up. But when the Muscogee County sheriff's investigator interviewed her, he was gone—that's all she knew. You had killed him, but all she knew was that he was gone—unless there was some evidence of a struggle. You put him in the trunk of your car and hauled him all the way back down here and put him in the river. He rode on his back the whole way and the lividity was fixed. We know he was drowned in Kayden's pool. There was chlorine and traces of chinaberry tree in his lungs. The bruises on his face and around his neck . . . You held him under."

He still doesn't say anything, but his face communicates plenty. The slight upturn of his eyebrows and the downturn of his mouth. Eyes averted downward, brow beginning to furrow. His facade beginning to crack. I'm getting through to him.

"I want to know why you did it," I say.

"I . . . I didn't intend to," Tommy says, tears filling his weary eyes. "I didn't even mean to. I just . . . You've got to know I wouldn't . . . I mean . . . I didn't . . . I wasn't going to do it until I was doing it."

We are in his office at the church, his Bible and notes for Shane's funeral on the desk in front of him.

"I just went to get him and bring him back and make him . . . I—"

"When you saw that Kayden was the beneficiary of his life insurance, you put it together, didn't you?"

"I had already been thinking maybe he swam over and broke into the houseboat, then when it turned dark climbed the hill and left. And that's what he did. He told me he had scuba gear tied up under the dock. Went under when no one was looking, got it, swam over to the other side, and . . ."

"So you drove up there to her trailer park . . ."

"He was out there alone, laying out by that disgusting pool," he says. "Kayden was at work. Good, hardworking people were in the river looking for him right then.

Megan was dead. Michelle and I were in pain like we've never known. And he's working on his . . . *damned* tan."

He shakes his head, narrows his eyes, looks into the distance, winces at what he sees.

"I couldn't believe it," he continues. "I just thought . . . who is this, this kid I raised to be . . . what had he turned into, what . . . We started arguing. I told him what I thought of him. The confrontation grew heated. He bowed up at me like the little badass Army Ranger he thought he was, but . . . I was so . . . mad. I mean . . . insanely angry . . . like pure rage . . . and I had this strength . . ."

"Why'd you kill him?"

"Am I talking to you as a chaplain or a cop?"

"I'm always both," I say, thinking of the small digital recorder in my pocket recording our conversation.

He frowns and sighs, but says, "I didn't do it because he was a coward. You're right about Carl affecting him. But it wasn't that he was scared of dying himself, though he was. The biggest part of it was him packing other sol diers' parachutes and them dying. That was going to be his job—a parachute packer or whatever they call it. That's what he couldn't handle. I didn't do it because he abandoned his country or went AWOL on his fellow soldiers. I didn't even do it because he broke the oath he made to our father, an honorable man who served his country with dignity and distinction and wanted nothing more than for his sons to do the same. I did it because . . . I didn't mean to do it. I didn't go there to do it, but when I did it, when I crossed the line I couldn't come back from . . . I did it for that poor girl and the hell he and our town put her through."

"Megan," I say.

"Seeing her shoot herself like that did something to me. It . . . I couldn't . . . And he was so unrepentant about it. So . . . It's like he . . . He was so casual about that Kayden girl, like . . . he'd done all this—had caused so much pain and . . . and Megan's death . . . and he was so casual about it, about the new girl and . . . having a baby. I have always wanted to have a baby . . . to have children . . . of my own . . . and he gets to and . . . he's so indifferent about it. I . . . I couldn't believe it."

He breaks down and begins to sob.

Leaning forward, he rests both elbows on the desk and drops his head into his hands.

"What have I done?" he says, his voice muffled from his crying and being spoken into his hands.

What so many do. Hurt those you love the most, those you expect the most from.

"Oh, God, I'm so sorry," he says. "Please forgive me. Please."

Grief is palpably present in the small room with us. I feel such sorrow—for him, for Shane, for Megan. It's overwhelming. Our frailties. Our failures. Our rage. Our outrageous actions and their severe and irrevocable consequences.

"What will my youth group think?" he says. "What have I done to them?" He lifts his head and looks at me, his eyes searching for something I can't give him. "They're the only reason I tried to cover it up. Only reason I haven't confessed yet. I just . . . I . . . I'm supposed to be their example, their . . . Everything I've told them, tried to teach them is a lie."

His actions don't change a single truth he's ever uttered, but I know what he means and don't argue the point.

He closes the Bible before him and pushes it away some.

"My plan was to do his funeral, wait a short while, resign, give it a little more time, let the church find another youth pastor and let the kids begin to build a relationship with him, then come forward and confess. I swear I was, I . . . would have."

I shake my head. "I don't doubt that."

"I . . . I still can't believe I did it," he says. "I keep thinking it didn't really happen . . . or that someone else did it. It's like . . . I keep trying to wake myself up from this nightmare I'm having, but I can't. I can't wake up."

He looks down at his notes and Bible again. Gathering his notes, his tears smearing the ink, he folds them, places them in his Bible, then pushes his Bible even farther away.

"Can I ask a favor?" he says.

"What's that?"

"Will you let me write a letter to the church and call Michelle and tell her before you take me in? Will you ask Anna to go over and be with her when I do?"

Chapter Sixty-one

Shock. Disbelief. Denial. Eventually begrudging acknowledgement.

The entire town is heartbroken.

Tommy had touched so very many people over the years—members of both the community and his church.

Kids in his current youth group, their parents who were in previous ones. Each in their own way express their love and support for Tommy. And also for Shane, Megan, and Amber—though these last three seem almost like afterthoughts to many.

Tommy's letter to his church is published in Merrick's paper.

The entire town mourns.

Funerals in quick succession—first Amber's, then Megan's, then finally Shane's.

The entire state mourns as more and more victims of Bobby Lee Banks are discovered.

Willard's free-labor foster kids program comes to an abrupt end when they are taken away from him.

As yet there is no evidence he or anyone else in the family were directly involved in what Bobby Lee was doing, but charges could still be filed for their role in aiding and abetting him—maybe even as accessories after the fact, but it's doubtful.

Time passes. People heal. Or forget. Or compartmentalize.

"I shouldn't be surprised or so bothered by it," Anna says, "but . . ."

"What?" I say.

It is evening and we are walking down Main Street, pushing Taylor in her stroller at a pace that is enjoyable but could also be considered exercise.

"Just that Tommy gets so much more compassion and understanding and forgiveness than Megan," she says. "People—some of whom contributed to her death—believe she is burning in hell right now while Tommy is a saint who just made a momentary mistake."

"Conditional love," I say, "fed through dogma and indoctrination. Try just suggesting compassion or understanding for Bobby Lee Banks."

"Hell, even I have trouble with that," she says.

Memorial Day has just passed and American flags are still flying from every light pole, flapping in the early summer evening breeze.

"It's so beautiful here," she says.

"More so since you moved to town."

"Have I ever told you how much I appreciate you taking every opportunity you get to say sweet things to and about me?"

I smile.

Back at our home on Lake Julia, steaks are marinating in anticipation of the arrival of Merrill and Dad, Merrick and Reggie, Michelle, and maybe even Megan's mom, though she was noncommittal when we called to invite her.

"Only three days until Johanna is back with us," she says.

"Counting the minutes," I say.

"It took us a while," she says, "but . . . we finally have the life we both always wanted."

"Yes, we do," I say.

"And the work you do gives us constant reminders of how very precious and fragile it is."

"It does," I say. "But I don't think we need them."

"No," she says. "I don't think we do."

And she reaches up to where my hand is on Taylor's stroller and puts her hand on it.

In that moment that is not enough for me, so I stop in the middle of our new little town, take her in my arms, and kiss her as if it's the first time.

"You did it again," she says, voice hoarse, hand over her heart, breaths coming rapidly.

"What's that?" I ask.

"Kissed my soul," she says. "You kissed me down to the very depths of my love-drunk soul."